The Secret Gardens of Mogador
Voices of the Earth

Alberto Ruy-Sánchez

THE SECRET GARDENS OF MOGADOR
Voices of the Earth

Translated by Rhonda Dahl Buchanan

WHITE PINE PRESS / BUFFALO, NEW YORK

Translator's Acknowledgments:
I am grateful for the assistance of the Banff International Literary Translation
Center at the Banff Centre in Banff, Alberta, Canada for a 2004 Banff
International Literary Translation Centre Residency Program Award. I had the
privilege of working there with master translators Margaret Sayers Peden,
Rául Ortiz, and Linda Gaboriau, to whom I am greatly indebted. I am also
grateful for support from the National Endowment for the Arts for a 2006
NEA Literature Fellowship for Translation Project and for grants from the
University of Louisville, which enabled me to consult with the author. Above
all, I would like to express my deep appreciation to Alberto Ruy-Sánchez for
his assistance, support, and friendship.

Publication of this book was made possible, in part, by funding from the
National Endowment for the Arts, which believes that a great country
deserves great art, and with public funds from the New York State Council on
the Arts, a State Agency.

Printed and bound in the United States of America.

First Edition
Cover photogaph: From the photographs of Lenhert and Landrock (c. 1904)

Library of Congress Control Number: 2008928421

ISBN: 978-1-893996-99-1

White Pine Press
P.O. Box 236
Buffalo, New York 14201
www.whitepine.org

Third Spiral

Gardens in an Instant

Fourth Spiral

Intimate and Minimal Gardens

For Margarita, Andrea, and Santiago,
my accomplices and explorers
of extravagant gardens

No one can be certain the body
is not a plant created by the earth
to give a name to its desires.
Lucien Becker

The dream over my flesh
moors its lilting island.
José Lezama Lima

The tree comes and goes in its shadow.
Adonis

The visible world is merely
a trace of the invisible,
following it like a shadow.
Al-Gazali

First Spiral
The Sleepwalker's Quest for a Voice

1. Dawn breaks, slowly . . .
and it was as if the light were singing

It was the hour in Mogador when lovers rouse, their dreams still entangled between their legs, behind their eyes, in their mouths, lingering over their empty hands.

Between kisses they fall asleep again. The sea roars at the sun, awakening them. But they open their eyes deep within their dreams, where they make love and delight each other, sometimes complaining as well.

It was the hour in Mogador when all the voices of the sea, the port, the streets, the plazas, the public baths, the beds, the cemeteries, and the wind entwine and tell stories.

In the Main Plaza of Mogador, a man traces an imaginary circle with his open hand and places himself in the center.

It is more of a spiral than a circle, emanating from his feet. He raises his arms to the sky and summons the winds. He hurls a purple veil into the air, compressing it first with his hands like a stone before casting it to the wind. It unfurls all at once and descends slowly to his waiting fist, like a returning falcon: a good sign. The invisible favors him.

He is the ritual storyteller, the *halaiki*. This morning his voice unravels like a cautious serpent slithering from its basket. And it becomes a hypnotic call in the air. A bird of prey that captures the attention of those passing by. Before long he is surrounded by young and old, women and men. The storyteller arouses new and old curiosities in each of them, and then introduces himself to all. He comes from very far away:

> I come moved by my blood.
> > By its music.
> I come guided by my tongue.
> > By its thirst.
> Every day I clothe myself with the winds,
> > the tides, the moons.
> And here, as you listen to me,
> > I strip all of that away.
> I am only the breath of what I tell.
> > A sleepwalker's voice.
> A voice feverishly seeking
> > the intimacy of the earth.

The crowd follows the *halaiki*'s gestures with their eyes and every breath they take. He looks at each one, then changes his tone and says, "Today I come to tell you the story of a man who became . . ." And he pauses as if another idea had crossed his mind, interrupting him. He turns to an old man sitting in the front, who looks at him in wonder like a child.

"Do you know what that man became?"

Then to another, further back, who lowers his eyes; to a woman who nearly escapes him; to a frightened boy.

"Can anyone tell me? I will give something special to the one who guesses. A reward, a surprise."

A group of young people decide to try their luck. They consult each other. One convinces the rest that he has heard this story before and boldly makes his way to the front to say, "He became a dog."

The *halaiki* shakes his head no. Everyone laughs and then all clamor to shout what they have been thinking. Each has an idea and a hundred spring forth at the same time:

"He became a fish. No, a bird. The wind. A woman. The sea. A stone. A river. Nothing. A mosquito. A dragon. The rain. A dream. A date. A pomegranate. A cat . . ."

The *halaiki* allows nearly all to have their say. Finally, he makes an abrupt gesture with his hands, demanding silence. He casts his gaze upon the eyes of everyone in the circle. He spins rapidly in the center, then stops and says slowly, "He became a voice. A voice that seeks to be heard with special regard by the one he loves, that desires to be sown in that intimacy like a seed in the earth. A voice that wishes to be fertile, sensitive to the earth that welcomes it, if it is received. This is the story of a man who became a voice so that he could inhabit the body of his beloved. Searching in her for paradise, for their unique and secret garden. That man had to face certain challenges in order to become that voice of the earth, but as fate would have it, nothing he achieved was lasting."

"This is my story . . . and nine times nine it begins."

2. Hassiba, the Obsessive Gardener

That morning I finally had to admit it. A strange obsession for gardens had taken hold of Hassiba. It began like any other fixation, with a strange, indecipherable expression. What was it that Hassiba saw when she stared so intently at things? I did not give it much thought at first.

Later she seemed to become mesmerized by certain flowers as if she were gazing at the sea or a fire. She wanted to plant trees in every corner of the city, and even along the streets. Not only did she wish to enter the interior patios of every house in Mogador that offered the slightest glimpse of a plant, but she also began to look at everyone and everything as if we were part of a garden in motion.

She would say that her friendships withered or flourished, while others became infested, and that certain people were flowers lasting only a day. Grafts, fertilizers, and cuttings were a few of her favorite words to describe all that she did and why she did it. In her eyes, the entire world had become the transcription of a great garden, the garden that contains all gardens.

One day I caught her sitting by the window, offering her skin to the newly risen sun: first her feet, then her legs, and finally the mound of her pubis, which she admired as if it were a bush, a forest, a sown field. "My plants are happy," she said smiling, without looking up from the tuft of unruly down on her belly. A new dark line seemed to be growing delicately toward her navel. She was content and quite serene, like someone contemplating a landscape that fills the horizon.

But I really began to worry the day she woke up shouting with excitement, just as the sun was coming up, "the great gardener has arrived." She opened the curtains enough to illuminate the edge of her bed and undressed to offer herself to the first warm ray of the morning. She stretched her legs gradually, spreading them ever so slowly, becoming aroused without touching herself, letting her breath and pubis sway along the tenacious sliver of light, as she made love to the sun.

I watched her in silence, alarmed and fascinated at the same time, trembling all over, jealous of the sun's slender fingers. Feeling that my hands were hopelessly cold as ice, I dared not touch her or even interrupt her.

Hassiba approached me slowly after recovering her breath, then still breathing deeply, she caressed my cheek, kissed me, and whispered in my ear with a low deliberate voice that her happiness was immense, that she had been in paradise, in the garden of the sun's fingers. I remained silent and awestruck.

That same night and the following days I tried to slip beneath the skin of the solar phantom who had made her so happy. It was a greater challenge than I ever could have imagined and one that would lead me to endure strange, almost inconceivable trials.

At times it seemed impossible to take the place of someone who was merely the object of her desires. It took a while for me to realize that I needed to transform my movements completely, my gaze, the way I listened to her. The music of my blood, the cadence of my caresses had to change.

Little by little I was able to grow a flower here, and a sprout there, but without truly creating a garden in her resplendent body. Undoubtedly, Hassiba's desire had risen like the midday sun in demanding ways that were completely unexpected, mysterious, and frankly, incomprehensible to me.

Then, I could not help myself and committed one of my most serious blunders. I began to tease her incessantly about her new gardening obsession, which Hassiba did not appreciate in the least. My comments became more and more offensive to her, although I was unaware of the harm I was inflicting.

A feeling that she was not understood was germinating beneath her skin, and she began to see me as more distant, incapable of sharing her concerns, deaf to her new voice.

Nonetheless, between one callous remark and another, I kept trying, without much success, to become the intimate paradise of this obsessive woman. Only once in a while was I able to do so. At the slightest hint of incomprehension, she would expel me from her body, from the realm of her body that was for me, undeniably, the real paradise.

3. A Secret Garden in the Eyes

I knew that two significant events in Hassiba's life had coincided with her blossoming passion for gardens, and I was certain they had kindled it: her unexpected first pregnancy, preceded shortly before by the death of her father.

Within a few months of each other, those two changes in her life had touched her body, causing the deepest sensations to emerge and subside within her a thousand times over. Rivers of pain and joy flowed through her simultaneously. She felt like fertile soil and sepulchral earth at the same time. But also we met and fell in love between those two moments. Her father had passed away five months before we first met, and his irreversible absence continued to grow within her, charged with intense, mysterious sensations.

She carried on by performing the smallest intimate rituals that could possibly invoke him. It took some time for me to understand the meaning behind all that she did. And, naturally I misinterpreted her actions, all of them enigmatic and fascinating to me. Amused, she let me believe for a while that my assumptions were true.

When I met her one autumn morning, it was like stepping into a secret garden where all things occur in surprising ways, where happiness is so complete that you wish to stay there forever.

I was walking through the old marketplace in the port of Mogador when I came upon a woman selling flowers in the most bizarre fashion, or at least it seemed so to me, for instead of carrying bouquets of flowers, she displayed just a few different colored petals in her impeccably tattooed hands. Apparently, her customers judged the merchandise and negotiated a price by the freshness and fragrance of the petals. Meanwhile the flowers remained at her house, in a somewhat secluded neighborhood, deep within the marketplace, in a nearly hidden interior garden that was impossible to see from the street; what in Mogador, I would later learn, is called a *ryad*.

It seemed to me that after she had completed a transaction, she would arrange to meet her customers at the Fountain of the Nine Moons, where nine winding alleys intersect or end, where the fountain's mosaic tiles cast nine different reflections of the waning moon. It was there that she delivered the bouquets and collected the money. From that corner of water, she would set out once more on her promenade around the market, with her hands extended, trying to entice the eyes and noses of those of us passing by.

When I came upon her for the first time, I had been

wandering a couple of hours happily lost in the unpredictable web of narrow streets. I experienced that rush of intoxication that labyrinths provoke by confronting us with uncertainty and making each step a threshold to a possible adventure.

I had dared to venture down the twisting lanes that assume a different formation each day of the week, depending on the presence or absence of those who fill the hidden plazas with their stands and merchandise. They say that even the merchants get lost in those nooks, where a different pattern entangles and unravels their steps over and over again. In Mogador there are always plazas within plazas, streets within streets, and shops within shops, and then there are the tiniest boxes of inlaid wood, marquetry boxes whose inner compartments can harbor, in miniature form, the essence of a marketplace or a forest: their fragrances.

Gradually I came to discern the universe embodied within every minute detail of the city. In Mogador each thing, each gesture, each sound is a door that unlocks other worlds. And very soon I was to discover that just as the vast flower and fruit markets may be contained in a tiny box of scented wood, one of the most seductive gardens of Mogador would reveal itself to me through the resplendent colored petals in the tattooed hands of that flower girl who had already begun to possess me.

But far beyond what I could have imagined at that

moment, in those petals a window was opening onto all my possible gardens of plenitude: a door to the heart of my desires. And perhaps in them lay the key to my destiny, that intricate blend of fate and desire that determines the course of our lives.

Before I ever crossed her path, she had chosen me as a potential customer, or so it seemed to me at the time. As soon as she saw me from a distance, in the streets of the marketplace, she came directly toward me. The expressive power of her gaze was intensified by her veiled face. It was as if she were shouting at me from afar with her eyes. She took about fifteen steps, entrapping me in her steady black pupils. But within a few yards of speaking distance, she lowered her eyes toward her extended hands. I saw the colorful petals, and without touching them, felt their texture of soft, perfumed skin. Those fragile petals contrasted with the meticulous geometric pattern tattooed on her hands.

She crushed a few petals with her fingers, releasing an intense fragrance that enveloped me. When she looked up, she no longer stared at me, but seemed to focus on something behind me. Then she stepped past me slowly, almost brushing me, without glancing back for a second to look at me again. She did this in such a way that the fragrance of her flowers, intensified by the few bruised petals, overpowered me, heightening her sudden indifference, obliging me, of course, to follow her.

Slowly she made her way into the labyrinth again. Although she did not look at me, she knew I was following her. Whenever I thought I had lost her, she would reappear before my eyes. The third time that happened I had come to a dead-end lane where there were no doorways for her to enter. When I suddenly found myself facing a wall, I turned to retrace my steps, and there she was, behind me, coming toward me.

Her subtle flirtatiousness turned bold, then playful again. In response to my questions, we discussed the price of her flowers and she told me about some very special orchids and cacti that exist only in Mogador, and about the henna plant from which the dye for hair and hands is extracted. Obliging my curiosity, she amused herself declaring quite seriously that it was better to sell petals on the street than entire bouquets because part of the allure of flowers comes from what they promise, from anticipation. Smiling, she told me it was the same with love.

I did not realize that she was nurturing in my imagination everything I desired in that moment. And between smiles she added extravagant details that heightened my delirium.

Later she explained the complex geometric design of her tattooed hands. She ran my fingers over the painted roads on her skin, and pretended, with one of her nails, to etch something on mine. But while she was drawing on my hand, something else became engraved in me that would never be erased.

Her very name was the resonant whisper of an incantation: Hassiba. Resembling a light touch, a laceration at the beginning of the word that becomes labial, almost suggesting a kiss in its final two letters.

She agreed to sell me a bouquet, which at first she absolutely had refused to let me buy. Finally, she offered the flowers as a present, but she did not give them to me yet, of course. We spoke until night fell, and with each passing moment, I wished more fervently that we would not part. In fact, I dared to hope the morning would find us together. But she had to leave and offered to show me her *ryad* the next day, but not before explaining the meaning of that magical word. Everyone in Mogador knows the word and uses it in different ways. To begin with, it means interior garden, a redoubt of nature inside a house. Furthermore, the house itself is called a *ryad* if it has a patio with plants. It also refers to any urban dwelling that offers an unexpected haven amidst the bustling streets. A *ryad* in the city is like an oasis in the desert. *Ryad* is, indeed, one of the names of paradise.

That is why the mystic Arab poets say a *ryad* is any special place where one may unite with God. Or that it is the union itself, just as the mystic Christian poets speak of entering the "flowering garden" to mean they have achieved the union of their soul with their beloved God.

The ancient poets of Al-Andalus, great explorers of

desire, whose conception of paradise is more sensual, even carnal, use the word *ryad* to speak of the capricious heart of their lovers: "a changing garden under the reign of the seasons." But also to refer to their treasured and mysterious sex, a promise of pleasures and a challenge for the gardener who patiently sows and tends it.

For me, in that instant, the word described this woman. She was her *ryad*. And her promise kept me awake nearly all night.

The word *ryad* rose to my lips over and over without ever tiring me. It was the sand of my hourglass, the measure of my insomnia. Hassiba had asked me to meet her very early at a place where the wall overlooks the sea: the Sqala, a very long terrace where the ancient cannons, once used to defend the port, still peer over the Atlantic. I arrived much earlier and watched dawn break over Mogador. The new light moved me as if it were a woman singing, her voice rising gradually, filling the horizon.

When she arrived, the sun was so low that her shadow was long and fresh. Drops of morning dew burst beneath her steps. From there we walked for a time that seemed both endless and fleeting to me. We took a route that was so complicated it would have been difficult for me to retrace. That path to her *ryad* seemed like a hidden opening in that point where time and space become mirrors and no one knows anymore what is real and what is a reflection.

As we continued on, I observed her slow and sensuous gestures. Strangely enough, I divined her body beneath a mountain of undulating fabric that spoke to me with each movement. This time she arrived covered with a *haik*, which is more than a veil: a very long white cloth draped over her kaftan, meant to be worn with a thousand pleats, and always held together by a hand, an unsettling reminder of its fragile permanence. A deceptively simple arrangement, deliberately designed to accentuate extreme reserve, but also extreme seduction. No doubt, in Hassiba's case, it managed to reveal with amazing suggestiveness all that it concealed: the alluring sensuality of a woman who was clearly and intensely vivacious, and brimming with desires.

We lingered in several shops, and she exchanged a few words with people passing in the street. She showed me places of strange beauty in the city, invisible to those not attuned to the curious forms that stone, wood, and streets adopt when weathered by time. Inaccessible spots I never would have known had she not taken me to see them.

When at last we arrived at her house, I was surprised to see that her shadow, so elongated before, was now hiding perfectly under her sandals, and the dew drops no longer burst under her feet for it was already noon. We had been together for many hours that to us seemed like minutes.

At first her *ryad* seemed to be a small, refreshing garden of fruits and flowers, unexpected amidst the narrow paths of a seemingly capricious design, inside an exquisite house decorated with tiles, another surprise within the alleys of the port. It was a second patio of the house whose flowers formed discontinuous lines of concentric circles, each more intense in fragrance and color than those before, like petals creating a single flower with the entire garden.

I had the impression that the whole house had been designed to showcase its treasure of flowers and that the surrounding city existed only to protect it, even its walls, the last visible petals of this secret *ryad*. The entire city took on a new meaning for me, as if I had fallen softly into an abyss of plants and wished to lose myself in it forever.

And in the heart of Mogador this woman suddenly became the center of the magnetic poles of this new world. I did not leave there again until she made the decision for me. For several weeks, which turned into months, I was her happy prisoner and lived in perpetual wonder.

I became familiar with the city, particularly its daily sounds that made their way to me through the latticed windows of her house. All the windows existed for listening to what was outside, more so than looking at it. And there were moments in which we lived immersed in the voices of the city.

I discovered that Hassiba took enormous pleasure in sounds. Not only was she enthralled by music, but even noises from the street sounded like a lyrical score to her ears, capturing her attention and fancy. She had me whisper in her ear a thousand and one different ways and told me that it was my voice that had seduced her when she first met me. I had the feeling that my entire body and all my gestures were for her echoes and modulations of my voice kneaded together. And at times, which I would recall later with unforgettable intensity, I sensed that one of her deepest desires was that I become a voice.

Those days or weeks or months I let myself be carried away by our mutual desire without thinking seriously about the future. I wanted to prolong the moment, and so did she. At times I thought, without much concern, that sooner or later I would have to leave. She became angry the two times I dared mention it, as if I had betrayed or wished to shatter the intensity that kindled our desire. I came to the conclusion that she would keep me inside there forever, loving her. And her possessive fury made me very happy.

Four months passed and then she became pregnant, exactly nine months after her father's death. My happiness was immense, and hers as well. To Hassiba, the new presence taking shape in her womb was an homage to her absent father, a powerful exorcism of his departure. I delighted in sharing that profound happiness with her, even more so when we realized that her erotic thirst had increased, some days with boundless limits. The range of pleasures that her pregnancy aroused became infinite. The flavors of all foods, especially that of fruits, and fragrances and sounds were surprising new delights. And all seemed to lead to our kisses and caresses.

Oddly enough, it was I who experienced most of the discomforts associated with pregnancy. I felt nausea, heartburn, and even the tempestuous cravings of the first three months. Hassiba told me that she had never felt better. At that point I believed nothing would detain or obstruct her extraordinary eroticism.

But when I least expected it, her desire for me diminished progressively, something I was incapable of understanding for a long time.

From those months of unbridled desire, of absolute paradise, I treasure not only the deep impressions her naked body left forever on mine, and the pleasures of her agile intelligence, so voracious and quick, but also a photograph.

That image accompanied me and offered some consolation when I was expelled from the kingdom of her desires. Holding that printed sheet in my hands, there coursed through my body such an avalanche of happiness upon remembering her and anguish over not having her that it took my breath away. I gazed upon that photograph obsessively, like someone with an addiction.

One morning, the ninth, she roused me with words rather than her hands or mouth, as she usually did.

"Do you want to know what I look like without tattoos?"

I told her no, that I liked her with them. They were tattoos made of henna, the dye extracted from the desert plant, which according to the Koran was found in paradise, next to the date and palm trees. Her tattoos formed an amazing geometry, like the perfect map of an ideal city, and I enjoyed losing myself completely in the narrow back streets of her carnal city.

It was also a way to be dressed in a robe of skin, a suggestion of nudity without nakedness. A cloak made only of lines, ritual lines, no doubt, that enveloped her in an almost sacred enclosure, where she was my new goddess and my consummate priestess.

As if she had not heard me, she continued to look for what she wanted to show me. From the bottom of an inlaid trunk made from the fragrant wood of Mogador's native thuya tree, she took out a beautiful piece of fabric folded several times to protect a photograph. It looked like a very old image, but it was impeccably preserved in an ancient frame. She appeared naked in what seemed to be a recent portrait. Only part of her head was covered by a pure white fabric with embroidered flowers, which I had seen everyday next to her bed and had even held in my hands. She had caressed my entire body with the fringe of that shawl.

Her dark, smooth skin contrasted with the faded, textured wall in the background. It was obvious that whoever took the photograph had asked her to raise her arms to accentuate the curves of her body. She holds them high but off to the side, with clasped hands. Her downcast gaze, also in profile, remains hidden. She offers her body to our eyes, but her discreet gaze conceals and protects her.

Her smile alone reveals a charming gift of wile and a great confidence in her sensual powers. The very same smile she had often given me during that time. I could tell that her naked body was neither tense nor relaxed, neither timid nor cynical. It was like her smile, an intermittent flutter of grace and seduction.

The photograph captured my attention during my amorous abduction, deepening my joy in infinite ways. Once again I remained mesmerized by that world of sensual paradoxes where a naked woman is dressed in tattoos and a totally clothed woman appears naked when she moves. Where a veiled woman shouts brazenly with her eyes, and a naked woman conceals them deep within herself. Where gardens are secret and secrets of ultimate pleasure are gardens: *ryads* of the soul and the body.

I asked when her portrait had been taken. Once again she gave me that snake charmer smile without responding.

Intrigued by her silence, I asked again and once more. Only then did she venture to say:

"That is my grandmother, not me. She and I share the same name, Hassiba, but her life was much more complicated than mine. Perhaps you would find it more interesting. When my mother died, I was very little and my grandmother took care of me the rest of her life. Her words were my refuge, her protective gaze my horizon. Whenever someone calls me temperamental or criticizes my unpredictable reactions, they say I take after my grandmother, that she planted the strange seed in me. To be sure, she sowed in my father the passion for gardening. An avid collector of orchids, she traveled constantly in search of them. She used to say that the orchid is the most seductive flower, the one that bears the closest kinship to human beings and the strange cultures they plant throughout the world. She made her home in the port city of Mogador and the mining town of Alamos, in the Mexican desert of Sonora, where my grandfather was born. But they also lived for a while in Granada. There, on the steep slopes of the Albaicín, she cultivated a Karmen, a terraced garden overlooking the Alhambra. My grandmother Hassiba told the best stories, and she wrote or transcribed some of them, but most of them she only told. I have many of her things and almost all her books. Later I will show you what used to be her bedroom. I have several photographs there, but in none do we resemble each other as much as we do in this one."

Hassiba's eyes shone as she spoke of her grandmother. The impossible desire to possess that image forever came over me, but I could not bring myself to ask for it. I convinced her to go with me to the house of the port's old photographer so that he could make me a copy.

"Fine," Hassiba told me smiling, "that way you will have me without having me. I will be a ghost living in the body of my grandmother that only you will be able to invoke. I will be like a new dream that you will awaken in a photograph taken long before the two of us were born: it will be our own private *ryad*, hidden completely in a time we did not live. A secret garden in your eyes. Only you will be able to see me though I am not there."

4. Another Garden within the Garden

Hassiba surprised me by revealing that the *ryad* I had visited was only the entrance to a much more expansive garden brimming with the unexpected. She said I had not paid enough attention to realize that, even though I believed I had reveled in every detail and delighted in all there was to see in her *ryad*. Then she explained to me that one cannot appreciate the gardens of Mogador by sight alone.

"Perspective rules in the gardens of other cities and often everything revolves around it. Both the feigned naturalness of the English garden and the accentuated geometry of French gardens are staged for the eye. The Mogadorian garden is created for all the senses equally. It is much more than a set arranged for the eyes. If you smell and touch, you will discover much more than if you just gaze upon it. If you listen and taste, even more."

I responded that her garden seemed very demanding, like her, but I would love to explore it. I had the impression that walking through her garden was like a trial, a ritual in order to be accepted by her.

"If you wish to see it that way. Remember that all of us, men and women alike, have our erotic rituals. No one surrenders before performing them. There are those who need certain words, sweet or violent, kisses, tender or deep, a special way of undressing, gradually or with great haste, a particular attire, mirrors, massages. . . Even the need for

38

nothing is a ritual that the erotic manuals of Mogador have always referred to as 'the empty ritual,' or 'the short-cut.' This garden is perhaps a long road toward me. Or toward you."

To enter Hassiba's house, we stepped through the ancient door of carved wood and iron rivets, and walked down several short corridors that twisted and turned, connecting to each other. They were completely adorned with tiles and could disorient someone with the keenest sense of direction. Walking through them, the compasses of the body would suddenly obey a new magnetism.

Then an interior patio welcomed us like an open extension to the sky for the lounges and bedrooms surrounding it on all four sides. Yet another adjustment for the senses: the most intimate spaces of the house opened to the elements, and while the inside faced outward, the outside had found its place within. The four rooms with three walls and a patio in the center were like an open fruit spreading apart.

All the walls displayed panels of tiles and stucco with geometric motifs. There were hours and hours of crafts-manship wherever one chose to gaze. A never-ending journey for the eye.

A hidden doorway in one of the corners of the patio invited us into a new labyrinth of corridors that led to another patio, this one full of plants: the *ryad* of Hassiba's father.

Every time I have been in this interior garden, I see it in a different way, as if it were one of those magical books that the storytellers in the plaza of Mogador recount, books that tell a different story depending on who opens them and what time of day it happens to be. At first I saw it as the heart of a flower whose petals were the house itself and the walled city surrounding it. Later I perceived this *ryad* as something else: a map of the world. Its four sections, divided by narrow channels of water, clearly represented the four corners of the planet. Each one featured regional plants from four different climate zones. At the center, in the navel of that world, was a fountain. Four streams of water tuned like distinct voices sang together at times, then separated into higher or lower tones before harmonizing again.

In the warmest area of the *ryad*, I allowed myself to be guided by an arid fragrance. It was carried by a light breeze that deposited salt on my eyelids and tongue, one that blew with much greater force somewhere beyond the *ryad*. And only then did I discover a new, nearly hidden threshold in the *ryad* that led us outside to a stretch of sand with scattered cacti and earth-colored stones. We found ourselves in an imaginary desert. The *ryad* from which we had emerged was like an oasis near the sand.

Palm trees covered one end of this desert land. The grove thickened, the further in we went, and its leaves eventually concealed the sky. The vegetation kept changing, embellished by ferns that appeared imbedded in the palm trunks, and a trickle of water flowed over a hidden slope, forming a pool in the shade. We sat at its edge to touch the water. Then Hassiba rose suddenly and ran toward what seemed to be an impenetrable tall hedge. She passed through it before I could catch her, calling out to me: "Find me without looking for me. Let your body's energy feel mine."

Alongside the spring, which Hassiba had run past, was a stone slab that seemed thousands of years old. On one side it displayed beautiful, ancient calligraphy like that which graces the entrance to the city's public bath, the *hammam*, but this one decreed:

> *Enter. This is the garden where the body moves to the wind like one more flower sprouting from the earth. Where the senses blossom. Where the dome of the sky and the geometry of the stars form a roof, a shelter for the flying pollen of dreams whenever they escape their reflection in the pools. Enter.*

There was no doorway behind the marker, only a barely

perceptible curved path that disappeared into the thickness. It was lined by tall bushes of penetrating fragrances. Each step I took delivered a different fragrance. It was a garden of aromas, some very sweet and others pungent, bitter, or quite harsh. Some were comforting and others strong. Without realizing when it had happened, that array of fragrances helped me distinguish other smells, and suddenly I thought I detected the scent of Hassiba's sex and could even determine where she had been. To my amazement, I could follow her even when the path divided into three.

I entered areas of the garden that seemed like different rooms. Some had pools and fountains. Others had only white flowers, while in yet another long and mysterious one, flowers of any color seemed forbidden. Even the foliage of the trees planted there was a somber green, similar in color to that of the trunks. Curiously, the very lack of diversity helped me differentiate the subtle tones of green, like those legendary color-blind men who can clearly distinguish eighty-one shades of gray.

In another area of the garden, a rectangular terrace was bordered on three sides by tall bushes with strange triangular leaves. On the fourth side was a stone wall from which nine jets of water spilled into an elongated pool. There the ground echoed my steps like wooden planks covered with twigs and dried leaves. After a few yards, I realized that besides the rustling under my feet, the ground generated yet another sound, as if my steps were piano keys setting in motion the different jets in the wall. The whole garden sang to the rhythm of my steps, confident or hesitant, serene or anxious. The garden was my echo or I one of its extravagant plants. I was one of its sounds.

Upon entering a high-treed terrace where the wind blew strongly, I lost Hassiba's scent. And yet something deep inside urged me to follow one direction and not another. It was that attraction, a blind magnetism between us that Hassiba had mentioned when she ran from me, daring me to find her. The very magnetism she had invited me to discover in this garden of infinite surprises, where my desire for her was entwined with nature, where I became like an eager root avidly seeking the dew.

Suddenly I saw her, standing there, waiting for me at the other side of an esplanade that ran along a very long and narrow channel of water. I was at the far end of that peaceful channel and she at the source, exactly where a round fountain, rising a few inches from the ground, gently spilled the water that eventually made its way to me, nearly one hundred yards away. I stood there, transfixed, drinking in her silhouette as if the magnetic power and tranquil beauty of the water extended into her body, ascending like a vertical fountain, a remarkable spring of my desires.

After a few minutes I decided to approach her. My lips quivered slightly, thirsting for her. I felt relieved to have her finally in sight and somewhat anxious because I had yet to embrace her. Then I noticed something slowly making its way toward me, sailing the barely still waters of the channel, an object she must have sent me before I could see her. On a mound of bark and dry leaves, she had placed a small filigree hand that always hung from her neck, the *hamsa*, or Hand of Fatma, a protective talisman that she now offered as a sign that she wished to share with me a part of her destiny.

I had wandered a large area of her garden for the first time without a clear notion of its size or its exact location in relation to the house. It was as if each space had opened within another exploring unimaginable depths and, instead of covering great distances, I had walked toward our innermost selves, toward the intimate space where I now felt united with Hassiba like a new graft, like someone implanted in the veins of the beloved.

At that moment I had the wondrous feeling that due to the strange effect this garden had exerted over my senses, I could finally draw nearer to Hassiba and be desired by her. I never could have imagined that this garden was the budding source of transformations that my absolute desire for her would impose on me.

44

5. The Tower of the Sleepwalking Phantoms

As we left the garden, Hassiba made me follow her. I thought we were returning to the *ryad* another way, but in the front corridors of the house, we stopped before an unexpected hallway that led to a narrow staircase. The shadowy darkness was strangely inviting. Something mysterious beckoned us to decipher it, like a veil, like a secret I wanted to discover at all costs. Hassiba took me by the hand and led me up the stairs.

"This is the room of the phantoms," she said. "Do not be alarmed if you hear something strange or if a clammy hand touches your back."

I imagined her grandmother's ghost waiting for us up there. Or her father's, disgruntled because the noise we made disturbed his sleep. Truth be told, it gave me little comfort to imagine this. Assuming her warning had been made in jest, I reproached her playfully:

"I thought you were taking me to the tower of the lovers, not the phantoms."

"All love stories are ghost stories. To be in love is to be possessed by another. When you desire someone, you become a house full of spirits."

We continued up the stairs and the darkness grew with each step. Our slow ascent, with eyes half-closed, gave rise to an eerie song that filled me deep inside and made my hair stand on end. For a moment it seemed unbearable to me, but we finally reached the top.

The light pierced us suddenly like a scream, and the disturbing song faded into a luminous silence. The objects in the room began to take shape slowly as they detached themselves from the whiteness that filled my eyes.

We were in the Tower of the Pomegranates, as suggested by the sign hanging above the door to the stairway we had climbed, a tile plaque displaying several of those fruits offering their seeds. Windows with latticed shutters opened on all four sides. There were divans below them, and books everywhere. And a table near one window, flowers in glazed ceramic pots, and on matching trays, among oranges, several pomegranates, one of them open as if someone had been there shortly before. There were also a couple of carpets with garden designs.

It surprised me that many of the books were about gardens. "Actually they are about gardeners," Hassiba corrected me. "My grandmother was a keen observer of anything to do with desire. From that to the love of gardens was only one step away. She admired all those who carried out their desires so fervently that they ended up expressing them through nature. She was mesmerized by incredible gardens and stories of orchid hunters, like herself. Even the avaricious tulip speculators of Amsterdam seemed interesting to her because of their exorbitant passion. These shelves are loaded with strange stories of obsessive gardeners who invested their wildest dreams in their plants, creating gardens no one had ever before imagined, gardens reflecting their senses. My grandmother used to say that my father became a gardener in this room as much as outside, in the garden itself. He was just a boy when, recovering from an illness, he began to read these stories and was struck by the desire to be like those gardeners. My grandmother claimed what happened to my father also happened to others who were transformed because of their intense, obsessive readings. Like Don Quixote who, after reading so many books of chivalry, set out to save Dulcinea and conquer giants, even though others saw them as windmills. Or like that worldly gentleman Ignatius Loyola who, while convalescing in the library of a castle where he read only about the lives of saints, grew so determined to be one that he ventured out into the world and became Saint Ignatius, founder of the Society of Jesus. My father left here with the desire to become a gardener and nothing could stop him."

Hassiba went to one of the windows and opened it, extending both arms. She stood still a moment, looking out and doing something with the branches that were knocking against the window, threatening to break it.

A dense smell of magnolias rose from the garden. And when the wind blew, that fragrance enveloped, bound and enraptured us. One of its swells enticed us to kiss each other, another pulled us to the divan and undressed us. Without my noticing it, she had picked a pair of blossoms from the magnolia tree whose branch was hitting the window. That tree held a meaning for her that I would discover much later, one that linked its flower to her father. At that moment her hands were full of white petals that she rubbed on my chest and neck and scattered over the divan. Our caresses and sighs were scented, and for a while, everything surrounding us had the intensity of that intoxicating aroma that will forever remind me of Hassiba and the lightly perfumed taste of her sex.

There I discovered a tiny mole gracing one of her vertical lips, between two folds that my tongue opened. I asked her, in jest, if her grandmother had one as well. Much to my surprise, she said yes, that several poets had sung its praises and that those poems were among her grandmother's secret joys. However, according to her grandmother, only one of the poets had ever really seen it.

"And what did the poems say?"

"That her lips were perfect magnolia petals between her legs and the mole was the trace of a distant star that had died so that she could be born. Another poet said the mole had sprouted one night during a full moon, when all the moments of admiration and all the stunned silences incited by her naked beauty had suddenly converged at that point. It was the permanent mark of her lovers' amazement. According to his poem, the mole was on her left lip, which proves he never saw it because it was definitely on my grandmother's right lip, just like mine."

I dared to suggest that perhaps the poet had merely been confused because he was facing her, that he could have seen it and made the mistake when he described her.

"Not according to my grandmother, and she had no reason to conceal anything."

"No reason that you know of."

"Say no more, or you will give me a reason to ignore you."

When the wind died down, when we recovered our breath and the silence returned, she continued showing me the tower and some of its secrets.

On a table were several photographs. In one of them, placed beside a tray of pomegranates, Hassiba's grandmother appears naked from behind, conversing in the sunshine with a friend. In another, surrounded by many people, the two women dance at a wedding reception.

"She was her best friend. Her name was Hawa. It was through her that my grandmother met my grandfather Juan Amado. He was desperately in love with Hawa, but it was my grandmother who ended up living many years with him, and they had my father. When my grandfather died, she wrote his memoirs pretending it was he who had written them. She published his story under a male pseudonym and many believed it. It was the tale of a man possessed by his desires, but seen through the eyes of a woman who had loved him, and perhaps understood and criticized him more than anyone. She composed the repertoire of his phantoms, nearly all of them 'typically masculine,' as my grandmother used to say. Some awkward and abusive, others intensely passionate and poetic."

"But my grandmother wrote many other things. And, when we were children, hungry for new and old stories, we would sit under the pomegranate tree, just outside here. And when my grandmother told a story, even the wind stopped to listen to her. She would open a space in time, as if suddenly a second were transformed into a mature fruit sliced in half, and in that enticing territory she would captivate us with the flavor of her words. Time was of no importance. She was the queen of time."

From a small box of inlaid wood, Hassiba took out a red fabric-covered notebook in which her grandmother had recorded her thoughts, recipes, poems, popular tales, and everything that had anything to do with pomegranates. She had made that fruit her personal emblem. She entitled it *My Pomegranates* and underneath, in smaller letters, wrote *My Whimsical Garden.* Hassiba read a few paragraphs to me at random:

"The pomegranate is ancient like the dreams of young goats and old poets. Its color sparkles like the silks of Samarkand. It stains clothing like the bloody remains of a battle on an open field and leaves in the eyes of whoever eats it the dazzling flame of lovers."

"It is an oasis fruit, a garden secretly cultivated within its skin. Like the intimacy shared in the body of the beloved. It is the fruit of the Sleepwalkers. In it lies the earthy voice of desire. That voice we sow and cultivate in our bodies and in those we love."

I asked her what her grandmother meant when she spoke of the Sleepwalkers. Hassiba told me about people who, perhaps without knowing it, have a strange disposition in their bodies that makes them desire, with absolute intensity, others possessing the same condition. Something like a secret caste with an insatiable sensual appetite. Not a secret society, but rather a way of being that is inherited and cultivated by people who began to notice their peculiarity many years ago. Their members recognize each other without ever having met, while those around them remain unaware. She told me about a physical condition that affects dreams and even movements. Then she reminded me of the occasions when, without really seeing each other, an extraordinary attraction had guided our bodies, one toward the other, as if something beyond our conscience had moved us.

"To be a Sleepwalker is to live as we do by the law of desire," Hassiba explained, "to live under the power of what is invisible in love. It is to listen and see something in the other that no one else can. To understand and obey the wishes of the magnolias, for example, as we have just done."

She went over to a bookcase in the back of the room and pulled out a volume, thin like a book of poems. It was bound in an aquamarine cover and filled with calligraphy inside and out. She quickly found what she wanted to read to me. Obviously she was very familiar with this volume:

"The Sleepwalkers do not distinguish between reality and desire. Their greatest, most tangible and corporal reality is desire. I move because I desire. Life with others is an intricate web of desires. The home a house of desires. The bedroom and the library are gardens of desires. In my garden my desires are braided with those of nature."

"But the Sleepwalkers do not become totally confused for they know very well that to desire is not the same as obtaining what one desires. They know that desire is always a quest. They also know that even though they search, they will not always find exactly what they yearn for. More often than not life gives the Sleepwalkers pears instead of apples, but they discover with great pleasure that they now prefer pears."

She interrupted her reading to tell me: "The Sleepwalkers are enemies of certainty. They know that everything changes, like a kaleidoscope, because desire molds us."

Hassiba took my hand and led me to one of the windows. The openings in the lattice were shaped like geometric pomegranates and through them a part of the garden at the foot of the tower was clearly visible. It was like discovering a labyrinth from above. She showed me a possible way out of the labyrinth. Then she took me to another window where one could see that the previous way out was a mistake and that another obvious solution was apparent. She repeated this several more times.

"It was here that my grandmother taught us not to believe blindly in our ideas, to accept that one can always be mistaken. Like you when you were certain that I was selling flowers from my *ryad*."

It took a while before I realized Hassiba was not selling flowers, as I had assumed. What she did with her hands full of petals in the marketplace was one of the many rituals she performed in those days to alleviate the pain of her absent father. She walked where they used to stroll together, carrying as relics some of the flowers he had planted.

When I finally understood this, I felt both insensitive and foolish. I asked her to forgive me. A deluded believer in all my fantasies, I did not question the meaning that I so rashly attributed to the strange and fascinating acts I had witnessed.

Once again, I realized how blind one can be in all of life's situations, especially when it comes to love. To understand anyone else is always a challenge. To comprehend the desired one is an adventure filled with misunderstandings, mistakes, and errors, sometimes fortunate, but most often not.

It is true that Hassiba had taken a certain pleasure in contributing to my misunderstandings and had even negotiated the price of the flowers that I had insisted on buying from her. But I had been an obstinate fool in my certainty. I begged her forgiveness and we laughed together. I asked why she had not told me the truth from the beginning.

"The truth," Hassiba said smiling, "is that you wanted something other than to buy my flowers. That was only your pretext to speak to me so that I could meet you. I could not take that from you so quickly. But that was also how you allowed me to see a fragile side of yourself, as if you had told me, 'I am a dreamer in your hands. Do with me what you wish.' Besides, that attitude of yours is very common and predictable. It did not take me by surprise. In Mogador, we learn as little girls that is one of the things men do. They take for granted that their assumptions are true and even fight for them. One of my grandfathers was that way to an extreme. Around each of the women he fell in love with, he spun a new philosophy of life, resolute and certain. It would collapse suddenly and then he would construct yet another certainty with a new woman. My grandmother Hassiba wrote about him and his obsessions in a book she called *On Lips of Water*. She presents the story as if it had been my grandfather who recounted his journey from one illusion to another, from one desirous certainty to the next. My grandmother used to say that her husband was a Sleepwalker, that he did everything like a Sleepwalker, especially falling in love. She criticized and

55

enjoyed him, with a smile, as I do you. Because you and I are also Sleepwalkers. I knew it from the moment I saw you in the marketplace and felt an attraction that took my breath away. I saw you open your eyes with the same thirst that sprang from mine. Between my legs there rose a feeling for you that filled me with joy and spread until it blossomed in my smile. We are Sleepwalkers who recognize each other from the first instant, like a seed that recognizes fertile soil and can distinguish in each element its somnambulant voice, its voice of the earth."

Then Hassiba put her cool hand under my shirt and touched my back. When she felt me shiver, first with surprise and then with pleasure, she said to me with a wide smile: "From now on I am the phantom that inhabits you." And she was absolutely right.

The wind stirred the magnolia tree again. Its touch moved us with greater force. There, in the Tower of the Pomegranates, among the sleepwalking phantoms, we obeyed its voice once again.

6. The Ritual of Flowering Death

Four months before I met her, Hassiba had attended her father's funeral wrapped in an air of absence, as if in a dream, like someone in disbelief who, at the same time, feels completely torn by the heartrending pain.

They buried his ashes in the garden, as he had requested. He did not wish to be thrown into the hole of death, next to the *hammam*, as is customary in Mogador, where the dead unite with the sea and return with the breeze to inhabit the shadows of things. Nor did he wish to be buried in the cemetery, which extends along the city's outer edge, near the little Eastern Gate leading to Marrakech, where so many await the Final Judgment.

He wanted to become earth, particularly the soil that nourishes the roots of a great magnolia tree that he had planted one day and tended, without imagining that much later he would desire to end within it. He wished to be transformed into something that coursed through its trunk, diluted in the flow of its sap, entering the veins of its leaves like a heartbeat. Something in the flower, in its sweet, ashen fragrance. Something carried by the wind that brings happiness to the living.

The women, dressed in black and white, formed a circle at the foot of that tree growing next to the Tower of the Pomegranates. All of them knelt down and began digging with their hands while they chanted and counted.

Each time they gathered nine fistfuls of dirt from the hole, they would raise their hands to the sky, like a prayer uttered with twists of the wrists and fingers. It was the painful song of their hands that accompanied their earthy, mournful voices:

> You let the dream seep into you
> like a river flowing through your veins.
> The dream of silence, of the longest night.
>
> And upon awakening, you left with the dream.
>
> We will bury what you forgot:
> your face without tears or smiles,
> your hands without strength or tenderness,
> your feet without steps,
> your eyes turned inward,
> your mouth without hunger,
> the cold that covers you like an invisible veil,
> the pain you no longer feel and leave with us.
>
> We will pass by here without seeing you.
> We will sit in your chair.
> We will sleep in your bed.
>
> Come speak to us at night in our dreams
> to make us feel that you have not left.

> The wings of the hummingbird you fed
> evoke you, cry out for you:
> your name will be written in the wind
> always never,
> never always.

In a procession through the city, the women sang while the men carried the body dressed in white, on a litter. Later, that too would be incinerated under his henna-covered body, along with the ritually torn clothing of those who brought him to his grave.

The image of his flaming body would remain in Hassiba's eyes for a long time, like a shining pain, like a blazing echo of the words he would never again speak, of the warmth of her father's lips and hands and eyes that would never again shower her with affection.

When a light swirling wind entered the garden, whipping a few branches, Hassiba was overcome by the feeling that her father was also there, his soul transformed into a breeze, greeting and bidding her farewell. A wind that mingled fleetingly with the dense smoke of the pyre making it dance for an instant, as if the gust had come to touch the new form his body was taking and abandoning in that very spot.

She reflected on how difficult it was not to take everything that passed before her eyes as a sign from her father, a form of his presence. Even the tips of the branches of a certain kind of tree seemed inhabited by him more than others. Hassiba did not understand why. And the very lack of understanding became a mystery haunted by the presence of the absent one. Everything suffered.

7. The Orphan Garden

Undoubtedly, Hassiba began to fall under the spell of the penetrating fragrance latent in certain plants that day her father died, leaving her his garden. Its ancient master, almost one hundred years old, had cultivated and enjoyed it for nearly nine decades.

Ever since she was a child, Hassiba loved to immerse herself in the hustle and bustle of the city and then enter the stillness of that interior garden, her father's *ryad*. For her, the contrast itself was always exciting: an initial shock to her senses, like entering a refreshing pool on an extremely hot day. Hassiba believed the garden had become an orphan, like her from that morning on, and now that he was no longer there, she decided to walk down every path, as one more of her farewell gestures.

Hassiba felt the need, like a ritual, to begin with one of the streets she had strolled with him hundreds of times, since she was very little. She decided to take the narrowest streets in the marketplace, the *souk*, where aromas and voices mingle in the air. The brilliant saffron shouted at her eyes. Men and women seasoned her steps with their hawking and bargaining. The light meandered through the crowd, planting kisses on the cheeks, foreheads, and hands of everyone in the streets. Skeins of freshly dyed yarn hung from arbors over the alleyways. Skins tanned at daybreak smelled like something very ancient, long forgotten.

That peculiar sky of hides and strands covered the alleys like a handmade cloud lingering there all day long. Camel urine, with that familiar smell, pungent and remote, had just begun to set the colors of the Berber rugs draped over the walls. She thought once again that in this marketplace, nearly identical to the *souk* she loved as a girl, flowers were missing. Those sold in certain stands were never as beautiful and impressive as the ones her father used to grow. So from that day on, whenever she walked through the marketplace, she secretly consoled herself by carrying handfuls of petals, as if some part of her father accompanied her. Those were the gestures that I had misinterpreted.

People who had known and admired him were quick to recognize this private ritual and greeted her with special complicity. At times they asked to see her petals and inquired about her garden. Often she would return and gratefully present them with an enormous bouquet.

When Hassiba explored every corner of the orphan garden, the day after her father would never again visit it, she sensed that each one of those plants had a unique relationship with the absent gardener, and she suddenly felt them clamor for his presence.

At first she thought that impression was exaggerated,

a reflection of her nostalgia, but she eventually came to the conclusion that her initial impression had been too weak. The relationship between that man and his plants, or between those plants and their gardener, was much more profound than she had ever suspected.

It was not the first time that she had heard of a plant becoming the living reflection of its gardener. She remembered a special plant marked by its owner like a fingerprint. One of her grandmother's many stories was that of Fatma, who departed Mogador leaving several plants in the care of a friend, among them her favorite, an immense impatiens bursting with red and white flowers and tender stems full of water. It was called impatiens because it turned toward the sun with amazing speed. One could almost perceive it shifting toward the outside whenever it was suddenly placed facing the inner darkness of the house. It was as if through the window someone beckoned and it spun around to respond to the shouting light.

Her friend cared for that plant as best she could, but nothing and no one could keep it from becoming languid, sad, pale, and finally perishing. The impatiens could not survive without Fatma, its absent gardener, and by ceasing to exist, it had found a way to follow her.

Hassiba knew that in a similar way her father had woven his life with that of his plants and that his entire garden was now like a mirror reflecting the man she had known best. That corner of nature had been molded over the years into her father's image. And now perhaps only she could decipher all those gestures of nature. But the idea that the entire garden could also die from sadness, in pursuit of her father, and suffer the same fate as Fatma's plant, made her feel dizzy, feverish, ill. It was as if she faced the possibility that her father could die twice.

For a few weeks Hassiba could not visit the garden. The mere thought of those plants grieving so blatantly over the absence of her father upset her. When she finally returned, she discovered that the plants had continued growing in a strange way. The subtle image of her father persisted in them, but they had taken on alarming traits, wild and unrestrained, as if something terrible in the personality of the deceased had literally blossomed in the plants and was screaming. The garden, so tranquil before, had turned into a wail, a laceration. And Hassiba understood that nothing could return it to the way it had been.

That corner of Mogador, which now flourished wildly, whose roots reached so far they broke through the walls, whose trees were vanquished by the weight of their fruit, was an intimate landscape that occupied her every thought, a song of lament she heard every hour of the day.

And a few months later, with that mournful voice infiltrating each heartbeat, Hassiba would shut herself away with me at night to sow and harvest caresses and other indescribable fruits of unbridled passion, as if love cultivated with a vivid imagination, a clear affirmation of life, would allow her to erase all the traces of death imbedded deep within her.

And in a way we ourselves had become plants in her father's garden. One morning Hassiba told me upon awakening: "Yesterday I dreamed that you tied your caresses to mine, and those knots were flowers sprouting from our bodies. They blossomed cautiously, then opened widely, and withered. Then we tried to make them appear again. In one night we invented all the flowers and fruits of our imaginary garden of caresses, and we also sent out roots that unite us more and more."

8. The Dream of the Shadows

At every instant, I was amazed to discover what our relationship meant to Hassiba. I never would have imagined the consuming presence of death lingering in each of our caresses, in each of our kisses, as if we were erasing inch by inch the heavy trace of his passing. The joy of our meticulous love and exhaustive lust struggled like an army of ants to devour the tiger of death sleeping within Hassiba.

I came to desire that in the darkness of night our somnambulant love would find the black hole of her absent father and fill that emptiness with its own body full of pleasure and life.

When Hassiba became pregnant, her transformed body implored me to listen to it another way. Her body spoke to me in a language of doubts, expectations, and silent gestures on her behalf. At times I was troubled by that mysterious relationship, oftentimes not knowing what to do or when to do it. Then I had a dream that was like a premonition of what awaited me.

I dreamed you were sleeping naked by my side, and that even before awakening completely I raised my hand to caress you. I touched the skin around your nipples and their texture enthralled me.

Moving in circles, I drew nearer to the hardest point, slowly arousing my fingers. Memory, the body's capricious queen, made my hand feel the sensations of my mouth.

The sun entered the room abruptly, thrusting its rays over your breasts. I even felt on the back of my meandering hand the warmth that touched you.

And the flickering shadow of a plant in the window also reached one of your nipples. It wrapped itself between my fingers, extending its caresses to your underarms. A subtle sway of that leafy shadow frolicked over your nipple and you seemed to respond to its touch.

It made sense to me that perhaps you could feel it because the shadow blocked the warmth of the sun. And so you were sensitive even to shadows and they touched you. I realized then that the shadowy leaves were identical to those of the flowers embroidered on your grandmother's white shawl, the one in the photograph, the one you had caressed me with. And this, too, made perfect sense to me. They are leaves of the same garden of shadows, I thought. The garden that can touch us in different ways.

Then I reached my hand toward you again but suddenly you were unattainable. You did not respond to the touch of my hand, only to its shadow, which had the same consistency as the shadows of the leaves and branches.

Everything merged in the shadow, and I had transformed myself into just another dark plant among the creeping vines. Even my voice, which rose toward you like another hand, became one more shadow in that garden.

Then I realized my hands could no longer touch your nipples, only their shadows. I moved toward you and encountered a new shadow that hindered me. In my dream, it was hard to accept that I had to transform myself totally into a shadow to really touch you. I had to change myself for you, according to your deepest desires, which little by little I was learning to decipher.

9. The Challenge

Hassiba's unexpected pregnancy had heightened all her desires. She knew that not all women reacted this way. But she shared that new capricious fever with a few of her friends, and felt fortunate.

Her body changed gradually, like a flower opening slightly more each day. All the flavors of food seemed to multiply in intensity and even water tasted much better to her. Her skin was more sensitive in the most unexpected zones of her body, as if the sense of touch had decided to dominate the others, and the crawling ant igniting the lips of her sex had continued its secret journey, descending suddenly toward her knees. Waves of desire traversed her, up and down, from her belly to her back.

I threw myself enthusiastically into exploring the new regions of her body and discovered a different woman each time, with new demands, moods, and dreams. Each day, the most ardent zones of her skin shifted, sometimes from morning to afternoon, and I have to admit that I was not always able to find them. Often, I did not even realize that the erotic challenge to listen to Hassiba and decipher the map of her desires had been altered.

One morning, when the sun stroked her ever so lightly with its radiant fingers, Hassiba lost patience with me, her other lover. Perhaps I kissed her in a way she considered mechanical, hurried, aloof. Hassiba awoke in my arms, but

I was unaware they had become the arms of an obstinate, predictable lover who did not understand that in each loving gesture one sows first and harvests much later.

She felt that I did not share her quest for love, her zeal for considering the best moments in life a privileged garden. Before long Hassiba was in another world, she understood another language, and communicating in it was like speaking with no one listening to her. She sensed that her whole body, her entire existence, was blossoming and gesturing frantically before the eyes of someone who did not even look at her. This was not completely true, but that was how she perceived it.

Suddenly Hassiba withdrew from my arms and declared emphatically with words that cut like pruning shears: "I do not want to have any more to do with you." Obviously surprised, when I realized she was serious, that sentence struck me like the blow of an ax, felling all the trees of my forest.

Seeing my desperation, she finally forgave me, but not before imposing a challenge, a condition that required me to be more sensitive to her body's constant transformations. After considering how difficult her request was that I learn to gaze upon the invisible and listen to the endless song in things, Hassiba decided to send me on a quest similar to one that appears in a story often told in Mogador.

"You should know," Hassiba told me, "that the *One*

Thousand and One Arabian Nights, which everyone here is familiar with, has a second part that is not as well known but just as fascinating. Do you remember how the daring and ingenious Scheherazade tamed the sultan Shahryar's bloody thirst for vengeance by telling intriguing stories that always left him anxious to listen on the following day to what happened next? Well, what many do not know is that in that second part, *The New Nights of Scheherazade,* time passes in her favor in an unexpected way. Not only does she capture the attention and curiosity of the sovereign, but also his heart and certain other parts of his body as well. She becomes pregnant and King Shahryar, day and night, takes great pains to fulfill her every whim. He even tries to anticipate them.

The most exotic fruits in all the gardens of the world are picked each night to please her. The most amazing music is composed daily to soothe her. The softest fabrics are spread at her feet by merchants who speak in very strange tongues.

Both content and insatiable, Scheherazade discovers that each day she desires more extravagant things and each night she desires her lover less. Her heart of hearts, which everyone knows is her sex, cools whenever King Shahryar approaches. But he loves and desires her so ardently that he is willing to do anything for her to welcome him back. And so one fortunate day, she finds a way for him to arouse her skin once more.

Although he is the king, he must obey the wishes of his lover and approach her humbly each night to tell her a story or she will refuse to receive him in her bed. Moreover, she warns him that he cannot use worn out devices of suspense, after all she knows them well, and unlike him, she will not be so easily satisfied with predictable stories.

The sultan is condemned to die of unrequited love if his offering of tales is not deposited ritually at her feet, or better said, at the ears of his beloved. In these *New Nights*, King Shahryar is converted into a new Scheherazade. Each night his private sovereign is seduced by his words. Not only are their roles reversed but the sultan is initiated by Scheherazade into the art of looking at the world in a more sensitive manner so that he may transform all that he sees and hears into stories that will rescue him from his misfortune, that will save him for at least one more night. Every time, one more night."

I asked Hassiba why she was telling me that story.

"Because I want you to go away and return with your sense of touch enhanced."

"What do you want me to do? I do not understand."

"You cannot touch me again unless each night you describe to me one of the gardens of Mogador."

"But there are hardly any gardens in Mogador other than yours."

"That is how it seems when you do not look closely.

Perhaps the entire city itself is a garden and we its carnivorous plants. The key is for you to reveal to me what you have yet to see, what you have not been capable of seeing. It is a question of listening more attentively. For each garden you bring me, a night of love. And only with an exchange of gardens will we make love again."

I felt that Hassiba could not have imposed upon me a more stringent amorous diet.

"They say that Mogador is not a city of gardens," Hassiba explained. "But if everyone refers to it as 'the city of desire,' it must also be the city of gardens, of the most secret and privileged ones. Find them for me. That is my greatest desire now. Before he died, my father told me that within all that we see is a garden, that in the fleck of dust floating in the light a garden awaits us, if we know how to appreciate it. He told me that the first garden of all the possible gardens in Mogador lies in the palm of the hand, always and whenever we can feel its intense, tingling sensation. Come and touch me with it, or never touch me again."

With that threat of erotic death, she offered the broadest smile she had ever given me.

"You are converting me into your Scheherazade," I told her.

"Into my storyteller at least, into a voice."

Hassiba told me emphatically that it was not a matter of finding the most obvious gardens and that I could not invent anything that did not exist or that the eccentricity of some gardener had not truly created in Mogador.

Crestfallen, skeptical, and burning with desire, I left to search for gardens. And I discovered that for me it was as difficult as going forth to name the winds, to identify the stars by day, or to count the stones in a swift river.

SECOND SPIRAL
GARDENS GERMINATING
ON THE SKIN

1. Paradise in a Hand

In a spice shop of Mogador, I began my search for the secret gardens of the city. The facade was decorated with glazed ceramic plates with intricate designs, each different, and each more surprising than the next. Against the white wall, they framed the three stepped rows of baskets and trays placed outside the shop as if wishing to detain the flow of those passing by. Each tray offered a small mound of aromas, forms, and colors, nine in each row. The reddish-orange saffron with its finely twisted strands seemed ablaze next to the dwarfed and pointed rusty clove. The ground peppers looked like rising dunes, and the whole peppercorns, stones from a turbulent river. But the queen of the spices seemed to be the henna, or *hina* or *henneh*. It was in great demand in its two forms. One basket showed off its small fat leaves, while a tray offered their powder, ground by a mill. A very concentrated pale green flour the women bought measuring their desires with a silver spoon that they dipped into the powder. And the sun beamed down on the shiny henna and lustrous silver with smiling complicity.

I lingered in the shop because the rows of colorful mounds made me think that, indeed, this was a garden, an orchard of aromas for sale. And in a certain way it was, but then I thought that behind this shop there must be an herb garden to visit, and that this place was what a flower stall is to a flower bed, not a garden but its display window. Not a paradise, but a sign that it is possible. Like what at first I believed Hassiba was doing with the petals in her hands to sell bouquets. Later, I realized that the floral geometry painted on each hanging plate and the entire collection on that wall formed another garden, or its design: a sketch of potential gardens, perhaps desired in dreams. Circles for the privileged eye to see.

The shopkeeper smelled of an alluring blend of anise and orange peel. He sauntered past his spices as if hoping to absorb their fragrances and then release them in the streets, like invisible advertisements for his wares. He called each woman who passed by "gazelle," a compliment they accepted with a smile.

I approached the shopkeeper without much hope, but asked him anyway:

"Do you have a garden where you grow your spices?"

"I have many, scattered throughout the world. The clove and cardamon come from India. The saffron from Samarkand. Those 'Leaves of the Winds' hail from China. The dried tomato tree from Colombia. The ephemeral morning glory is a flower from Costa Rica. That hot pepper called *chile de árbol* comes from Mexico. My garden is everywhere. The four walls you see are invisible. You need only smell my spices and their fragrances will carry you around the world."

"What I really wanted to know is if you have a garden

in Mogador or know of someone who has one, other than the garden of Hassiba's father, which I have already seen."

"Within the walls? No."

"But they say the origin of all gardens is right here in Mogador."

"Did you buy that garden? Did someone sell it to you like those Americans from Texas who were sold the Eiffel Tower? If you want I will sell you one of those gardens."

"No. I just want to see it."

He made a face indicating his ignorance and called out to a woman in the shop, a client he knew by name. He asked her my question. She also smiled, but without mocking me, and said:

"I know what kind of gardens you wish to visit. The kind that merchants like this man call The Gardens of the Gazelles, where love is cultivated and at times jealousy is harvested."

She extended the palm of her hand with a gesture of pride and seduction. It surprised me. Her henna tattoos were like Hassiba's but with a different design covering her hands and part of her wrists and forearms. Its apparently simple pattern was very complex. There were separate shapes with passageways between them. She told me that particular design was called "The Garden of Origins": "Wearing it, we are reminded that each day we should build paradise with our hands. Here is inscribed our duty to make the days pleasant for those around us and for ourselves. And that we should pursue our desires with the will of a closed fist.

It is also a talisman that protects us from evil forces. The city has its walls, we have gardens in our hands. They serve the same purpose: to protect us if necessary and provide character and beauty if protection is not needed. Our garden also charms, hiding part of our body, while calling attention to it with alluring forms that catch the eye like the feathers of a peacock. It is like latticework over our body: it conceals us while suggesting that something valuable is hidden within. It enhances beauty, letting it enter the dreams of our admirers. Evoking the beloved, men always remember the first garden of henna whose pathways are a labyrinth of promise. For this reason, it is worn by the bride.

And many times there is secret writing in this miniature garden. Indecipherable words that cannot be read, but when touched reveal how to be happy and how to possess all the beneficial powers, such as how to please lovers and oneself, how to ward off the evil eye, envy, conspiracy. A medical treatise from the eighteenth century claims that 'henna has ninety-nine virtues, but the primary one is happiness.' Naturally, it is a *hamsa* and it heals. It tells us how to find paradise each day, avoiding the tortures and pleasures of evil, and how to become, with the entire body in motion, the music of that journey to paradise. An ancient Mauritanian poet, Habib Mafoud, used to say: 'henna is serenity. And if the soul had a color, it would be the color of henna.'

All this is found in the actual dye extracted from henna because it is one of the trees, or rather, bushes of paradise. It is a desert plant. In it lives the memory of the first rainfall. It is resistant to everything because it was present at the beginning of all things. Everything in the world originated from a henna bush. They say that the animals, all the animals we know, are descendants of a plague that befell the henna leaves. And the scent of the henna flower is the origin of all the seductions in the air, of all attractions, of all desires. And therefore, of all human beings, given that we are children of desire and inhabitants of the air, water, fire, and the garden. The original garden is reborn each time we draw it on our hands with henna."

That is how I wish to trace on your skin, Hassiba, the secret geometry of our paradise. A figure that only you can see and decipher in a language invented by our bodies. With lines and forms that will never allow you to forget each sensation we felt as lovers. I want to be the inscribed line of happiness on your skin. To engrave you with the fleeting wake of my fingers caressing you, with the invisible ink of my saliva traversing you, with the trail my eyes leave when they look deep into your face or between your legs. I want to be the henna that covers you and comes from that place beyond the world that we shared for one instant.

2. The Garden of Dancing Spirits

In Mogador's musical instrument shop, which Buzid inherited from his grandfather more than thirty years ago, the best goat skin drums in the city can be found, although everyone agrees that those made from fish skin are better.

The goat skin drums are tuned over fire, rapidly, but go out of tune just as quickly. People say they are capricious like the goats that climb the argan trees on the outskirts of Mogador and only come down when they feel like it. They say the drums have the appetite of a goat. The heat of the music is enough to tune the fish skin drums, and the echo of the hands that traverse them resonates for a long while. They only go out of tune from abandonment, during the empty silence that replaces the dense quiet, present for days after the festivals end.

In Buzid's shop there are flutes made of wood, stone, and clay, also metal castanets, and several kinds of lutes, guitars, *rababs*, violins, and other string instruments. There are cylindrical drums made of clay and tin, and others that are round wooden boxes resembling large tambourines. And there are square tambourines, covered in skin on both sides and played back and forth, as if bitten by hungry hands. These are tattooed with geometric figures, flowers, and Hands of Fatma that are also covered in tattoos.

I asked Buzid what he knew about the tattoos on the instruments. I was curious to know if they were merely decorative or had ritual meanings. He led me to the back of the shop, and in a bookcase filled with ancient unbound books, some notebooks, and loose folios, he found about twenty sheets, deteriorated from age, which had been drawn by his grandfather. On these he had sketched some of the famous tattoos for instruments from Mogador.

There were several on each page, and those that seemed most beautiful and intriguing to me were the ones with the inscription "Garden of Spirits" written below, next to the name of a musician in Mogador who was well-known at the beginning of the century. Another note mentioned they had been tattooed on an instrument called the *gambri*. I was anxious to see that instrument played. It was in the possession of a descendent of the man who had painted it and would be played in the great ceremonial festival taking place that night. Buzid introduced me to the *gambri*'s new owner, who would preside over its tattooed Garden of Spirits.

The instrument is a very ancient type of guitar with a walnut wood sounding board, which is covered on the front with goat skin and sits under three mighty strings that make it vibrate. The wood has a curved shape called the "donkey's back." From this extends a round wooden arm with strings attached at different heights. The most famous *gambri* of Mogador is this one, tattooed with unique garden motifs on the surface of the skin that resounds ritually beneath the three strings. The *gambri,* known by some as *hajhuj,* is one of the typical instruments of the *Gnawas,* ceremonial musicians organized in brotherhoods. They are the survivors of the black African immigration to the Islamic world. Their music and rituals are like those practiced in Cuban *santería,* Brazilian *candomblé,* Haitian voodoo, and the Garifuna invocations. All the ritual Caribbean music that blended the worship of African spirits with the worship of Christian saints are sisters to the Islamic music that fused the same animism with the adoration of Muslim saints.

The patron saint of *Gnawa* musicians is Sidi Bilal, an ancient Abyssinian slave and the first *muezzin,* the one chosen by Muhammad to sing the call to prayer from the high minarets. According to legend, his remarkable voice was the only thing that could lift Fatma, the favorite daughter of the Prophet, from her deepest abysses of melancholy.

Every *Gnawa* group has a *maalem,* the same title given to master craftsmen. Each of the other musicians in the group is either a practicing artist of this ritual music or an apprentice to the *maalem.* The *gambri* is his primary instrument. At a crucial point in the ceremony, he puts down whatever he is playing and picks up the *gambri.* The unique sound of its chords is heard as a deep, tranquil force amidst all the sounds. Surprisingly, it is more powerful than the drums, castanets, and voices of the musicians. Perhaps this is why it changes the sentiments of the crowd and generates another dimension for the ritual, no doubt setting the stage for those who will enter into a trance. It invokes with a voice of authority the souls and saints who will take possession of the bodies of certain participants.

The *Gnawa* ceremony begins in the street. It is a procession and carnival, led by bands of musicians, with large drums and castanets, who sometimes carry a sacrificial lamb adorned for the festival. After the sacrifice, the group goes down the street singing and dancing. The procession grows and the people behind them multiply. The musicians dance and all those behind them as well. They stop in a few plazas and then continue on. The musicians ask the prophet Muhammad and Sidi Bilal to bless them with *baraka*, good fortune for them and the participants. The *gambri* does not yet join in.

The procession arrives at the house hosting the ceremony, where its mistress welcomes us with dates and milk. We all enter the patio where this part of the ritual continues and ends. Then come the games: part of the ritual preceding the possessions in which the musicians perform symbolic movements, acrobatic feats, parodies of traditional African spirits: Gri, the mythical hunter of wild beasts, and Buderbala, the mystical wandering beggar.

Then the *maalem* is presented the tray of incense and perfumes. He lights them and passes his *gambri* over that fragrant smoke. The voice of his purified instrument transports us to another dimension. According to the *maalem*, this is where the Garden of Spirits appears. Suddenly we are in a mythic forest where the powerful souls reside. Each possessed spirit has a corner there, and a particular geometric symbol on the *gambri*'s skin. Likewise, each has his special color, its *melk*, or distinctive musical theme, and his own dances of fortune.

The *maalem* invokes the spirits with his ritual, compelling music. Later, its resonance becomes the channel through which the souls navigate from their world to ours. Entranced by the music, they take over the bodies of those who listen with open mouths, with legs ready to spring forth dancing, with eyes open to the wind like windows without shutters, with bones turned hollow and airy by the ritual dance that moves them. When, under the spell of the *gambri*'s voice, the spirits enter the blood, dancing to their rhythm, the possessed person loses his own cadence and no longer controls the beating of his heart. The practitioners tie his waist and chest with colored fabrics, according to the color of the possessing spirit, and hold him from the tips of the material to prevent possible harm when his muscles become completely loose and shake uncontrollably.

Only the *maalem* knows how to play the chords to invoke a possession. The garden on the *gambri* is the invisible temple of the *Gnawa* guild: it cannot be seen, only heard. It emerges from the void like a supernatural apparition. When the garden does not vibrate, the spirits sleep in the other world. When the ink sown on the *gambri* vibrates, the garden of symbolic flowers and spirits fill the air, entangled in the music. The garden of the *gambri* is one of the essential places of Mogador, as important as the *hamman* or the public oven. Without a doubt, it is the most sonorous of its secret gardens.

Listening to the Gnawa music, I think of the invisible, shifting map that guides my hands over your body. And it is your voice, moaning or crying or breathing deeply that tells me where to find the spirits today who awaken in you at the touch of my fingers. You orient and disorient me, and in your garden of spirits, I lose my way. Reeling, I shout under the spell of your hands and possessive mouth. When the powerful voice of your corporeal gambri, the three tense strands of your sex, rises and blends with all the sounds that are and ever were, you also course through me like a voice beating stronger than the most aroused blood. The blood that arches bodies and throws them uncontrollably into the darkness of your garden of souls. I want to be sown forever by your voice, and to live in the garden of your sighs, of your silences teeming with echoes.

3. Paradise in a Box

Many Mogadorians earn a living from woodworking, especially carving the fragrant thuya tree whose roots are like the deformed fingers of an immense hand plunged into the dunes. A well-known legend in Mogador explains the origin of the thuya groves surrounding the city, and also speaks of the craft hewn by rough hands, forever scented by this wood. I was fortunate to hear this garden story on the breezy terrace of the Taros Café. And I recount it as it was told to me.

It is said that the very sages and architects who designed and built the famous labyrinth in which Abenjacán el Bojarí may have died (according to a respected *halaiki*, a wise, blind storyteller who dreamed about tigers and mirrors), were later charged by their king to build a perfect garden. They drew up a plan that followed precisely the sacred descriptions of the supreme model of all gardens: paradise. First they established the four classic sections of diverse vegetation on different levels, clearly separated by channels of running water symbolizing the four sacred rivers: one of water, another of milk, one of honey, and another of purified wine. They incorporated infinite displays of water that sang at the foot of the pomegranate trees, along the corridors of coconut palms and date palms, and amidst the wild henna bushes. They erected pavilions, patios, and wide pathways that invited relaxation, contemplation, and encounters, all designed and laid out in such a way that made it difficult to tell if one were inside or outside them.

They also chose a gardener. After searching far and wide, they found a man among the artisans of Mogador who seemed in his life and work to be a lover of perfection and nature. He was also patient, intelligent, and bold. He worked with the roots of the thuya tree, native to Mogador, making furniture and objects that amazed everyone. To transform him into not just a gardener but the best one of all, the three wise architects touched his head ceremoniously, each bestowing their own dominant passion upon him like an extraordinary legacy. And so, while he continued to nourish his inherent qualities, the new gardener became possessed by three great passions. The first architect, a great hedonist, transferred his excessive zeal for flowers to him; the second, the most skillful, infused him with the pleasure of working tirelessly with his hands; and the third, the holiest and most assertive of the three, transmitted his incredible passion for geometry, assuming as well that because of its perfection, geometry was, without a doubt, the ultimate manifestation of God.

Their masterpiece complete, the wise architects, each more than one hundred years old, could retire to die peacefully in their village far beyond the Sahara, a distant place that was inaccessible without magic, and whose earth was so full of powers that everything was built of clay but endured as if made of stone.

For nine years the gardener cultivated his garden

patiently and skillfully, achieving amazing results. His flowers were recognized around the world as the most beautiful of every species. The required cycles for the fruit trees to reach their peak had been completed in exactly nine years with great success. Moreover, every corner of his garden was a place of unexpected repose that offered visitors a feeling of the infinite because of its daring and subtle geometric composition.

That spring his happiness was as deep-rooted as the splendor of his garden and lasted throughout the summer, enduring as long as the intense green of the leaves.

But in the autumn, little by little, a cloud of sadness crept into his days, accompanied by a growing dissatisfaction. He realized his garden was far from perfect. And so he began projects that accentuated the geometry of bushes, rows of trees, and domes shaped by their intertwined branches. Into the long channels of running water, he inserted breaks that created a labyrinth.

Every day he would rearrange the plants and structures in his garden into obvious geometric patterns. He dreamed about abstract forms that sprouted from each other like fantastic plants, regenerating themselves according to a perfect equation. But awakening lead only to disappointment. He became exasperated by the unwillingness of certain flowers to resemble the designed flower of his dreams.

One day he cut all the flowers. The king was away on a trip and no one else could stop him. The garden was his kingdom within the kingdom. And the king's journey would last at least one year.

Another day he chopped all the tree trunks converting them into octagonal columns. With the thousands of meters of stripped bark and wood, he had a wall constructed to enclose his garden completely, blocking it from view of the scandalized courtesans. Neither he nor his assistants left the garden for months. They had plenty to eat in the orchard. The white-tailed deer and the striped rabbits, which had made the place famous, also disappeared because of the nutritional needs of that small battalion of gardeners who took turns working day and night.

For nine months there was no silence or rest inside the woven wall. One day nothing could be heard and everyone in the kingdom became anxious. Rumors spread about what had happened. Some swore that everyone had committed suicide and their remains served as fertilizer for the plants, or that the crazed gardener had buried everything, convinced the trees would grow in the opposite direction, downward.

One day, without any notice, the king entered his city. He had returned sooner because of the alarming messages concerning the mental state of his cherished gardener, which for the past few months had been waiting for him in each new place he visited. He imagined he would find his garden burned to the ground and his gardener hanging from some branch. After presiding over an enormous public celebration of his return, the king summoned the geometric gardener.

He welcomed the king back, and while greeting him, his excitement grew proportionately until he could wait no longer and announced that he had a surprise for him, that at last his garden was perfect.

The king felt more at ease and decided that all the rumors about his gardener were the result of envy in the court. It was not the first time this had happened. The gardener was fine and tending the garden with his usual enthusiasm, like someone possessed by the life of his plants.

As they walked together toward the closest of the twenty-seven gates in the garden wall, the king spoke with amazement about the gardens he had seen on his journey.

"But do not worry, I have no doubt, you remain the best gardener in the world. In spite of all the efforts made by others, not even the most marvelous garden I have seen comes remotely close to ours."

When they reached the gate, which the king had never seen closed, the gardener pronounced a numerical password and one of his assistants let them enter. The king nearly fainted upon seeing his garden suddenly reduced to a heap of plants, half-uprooted and torn to shreds. An arid reserve with chaotic mountains of wood piles.

"What happened to my garden? This is what you call a perfect garden? There is nothing here but desolation and destruction."

"What was here before was barely a sketch of your perfect garden. It only served to become what you will now see."

The geometric gardener gave an order by clapping his hands, and five assistants appeared carrying a beautiful cubed box made of different precious woods inlaid one within the other, an art form known today as *taracea*, or marquetry.

"It smells like cedar. Did you cut down my favorite cedar trees, the arz that I had transplanted here from the Atlas mountains? Did you chop up my cedars just to make a simple box?"

"It is not a simple box. The geometric pattern on which it is based is the precise design of the most beautiful garden in the world. All of its proportions are exact. Paradise must be like this. It is a perfect object, the image not only of paradise, but also of God. The main frame had to be made of cedar from the Atlas mountains, the arz, because it is the only wood that takes many years, sometimes centuries, to understand that it has been cut, that it has been separated from its mother and has been given freedom. Its soul stays green and fresh for decades. Also, the fragrance of cedar contains the 'essence of happiness.' Anyone who suffers from anxieties of the heart need only sink his or her nose into a box made of this wood to be happy again. Arz is used in the public baths, the *hammams*, because it is not weakened or deformed by humidity nor is it affected by changes in temperature. And it is resistant to attacks by plagues of insects, unlike other trees so hungry for love they allow themselves to be devoured.

Its only imperfection occurs when it is rooted in the earth because, under its influence, it has the false impression of living on its own, out of control, and becomes deformed in strange and irreparable ways. Undoubtedly, its best form of life, its greatest expression, is seen in the impeccable geometry of a cube with rows of other woods inlaid at precise distances, thus revealing its exact proportions and multiplying the image of its perfection. This marquetry box is, my king, the enhanced synthesis of your garden. The perfect expression of nature. It is the tree, not reduced but elevated to the purest geometry possible."

The king took the box in his hands, opened it, feeling a burst of balsamic fragrance enveloping his face, and smiled broadly.

The gardener was pleased that he had convinced him. All his effort had been worth it. Now even the king would recognize that the garden of all gardens was contained within that box.

But the king was smiling because he had finally decided what to do with that stubborn gardener possessed by a geometric delirium.

"You arrogant man, you were a master, a remarkable *maalem*, a great artisan, and that was not enough. You believed you were God, and for this you will burn in hell. Today, before the sun sets, I will place your ashes in this box."

And they say it was from that passion for gardening that

the art of *taracea* was born, the art of inlaid wood that spread from Mogador throughout the world.

But they also say that after a few months, from the little mound of ashes sprouted a beautiful and noble plant. Not an Atlas cedar, an arz, as they expected in the court, but rather a Mogadorian thuya, like those surrounding the city to the northwest, anchored in the dunes that used to invade the city whenever certain winds blew.

Taking leave of Mogador by the dirt road that goes to the port of El Jadida (the ancient Mazagan), one gets the feeling of sailing across a green sea. The thuyas are low enough to see their shimmering treetops rippling like endless waves in the constant wind. They say that the wind is the spirit of the perfect gardener, imprisoned in the natural imperfection of that forest from which he tries to escape.

Let me resuscitate in your dunes and anchor them with my roots. Let me smell in your perfect box everything about you that captivates me. Let me feel you inlay me with all your woods. Let me be the proud prisoner of all your movements. Let me admire you as if a thousand forests and seas and deserts had adorned the iridescent perfection of your beauty.

4. The Garden of the Invisible

A frenzy of savors from around the world converges in the spice market of Mogador. From the somber and austere black pepper to the capricious paprika; from the spectacular star anise to the deceptive insignificance of the slender dill; the inevitable seduction of cinnamon, clove, cardamon, and vanilla; the noble presence of garlic and onions; the indispensable mustard grains and perennial sesame seeds. Hundreds of sensations for the tongue present themselves, filling the eye with unexpected colors, intensified by their aromas and textures.

The extremely sensitive are not allowed to walk through this part of the market. Children are warned about the vices of the senses that may be acquired here. Women know that germinating here are the experiences of the palate that weaken the brain and heart.

Also located in this part of the market one may find the traditional apothecaries with their dissected bird wings, bat tails, fresh and dried mushrooms, dozens of amulets and potions, and even some newly released pills.

Between a mountain of saffron to the left and a strand of vulture wings to the right is a simple stall with an engraved sign advertising the shop's name: "The Garden of the Invisible."

There is something intriguing about its ancient plants, preserved by the woman who owns the shop. They do not look like the old dried plants one would expect to find in any herb shop. They seem to have been dipped in a liquid that evaporated a long time ago, perhaps to better preserve them. They are cared for with veneration, as if there were more to them than meets the eye. Some are still poisonous, while others may provoke diarrhea or soothe toothaches and headaches.

Their mistress tells me that each one of these plants is powerful, that "one must be very cautious with them." I ask her to please tell me about their magic, what they cure or what harm they may cause. She says it has nothing to do with that, but she refuses to waste time explaining to me something I will undoubtedly not understand. All that she will tell me is that these plants are from the Garden of the Invisible.

"And where is it? I want to visit it."

"I assure you that the Garden of the Invisible cannot be seen with your eyes. It is the place where good and evil plants grow and acquire their powers before coming here, where we can see them. Some seeds open the door in the earth that leads to the invisible and a plant enters through it. Because the doors are so small, only the tiniest enter, barely noticeable among the other plants. I care for them, but they do not always grow. Some have their own will, their own powers. They have *baraka*. Some flowers may stink to us, but that scent may be wonderful in the world of the invisible. Likewise what we consider pretty here may not be there. Look at this."

Then she showed me a dried flower that looked quite ugly and smelled terrible as well. "This one is among the most revered."

"There?"

"There and here. The invisible is also among us. Those who calculate everything and label plants with first and last names do not wish to see it. But the invisible is like a thread that runs through us, making us fall in love, become gravely ill, or binding us to something or someone. It is not good to have loose threads (invisible ones, mind you). In Mogador we call it *baraka* or *nesma*. But something similar exists in other places. A woman who was here a few years ago told me that the ancient Americans used to call the power of the invisible *tonalli*. She told me that people died from losing it and that maintaining its fervor was a life-long challenge. It is the invisible in life, not a soul, a narrow concept, but more than that because it is the soul and the body and all that encompasses them. Nor is it only something that heals. It is the life force itself. Naturally it is not recognized by doctors because it seems that modern medicine does not like what cannot be seen. Some flowers make a pact with the invisible and control what is invisible in humans. It is a secret circle. Inevitably chilly drafts present the greatest danger. Everyone dies from them even though some will say it was from something else. The plants you see here combat the cold. They carry the sun within and transfer it to people, planting it in their chests.

The Garden of the Invisible? It is everywhere and what we see is only a speck of what is behind or within these flowers. Obviously no one can say what it really is like because it has never been seen. But it can be felt. Those who have embraced the invisible with feverish curiosity have not returned. Not yet."

That is how I wish to travel from my world to yours and never return unless with you. I want to make a pact with the most invisible part of your body that beckons me from within. I touch and smell in you what so often is not seen. My hands and mouth feel their way blindly, searching for you. Truly I believe in the invisible in your body even when you are so close that I no longer can see anything. If I am sad or weak, you heal me. The greatest danger to us is also the chilling cold. If that force, baraka *or* tonalli, *abandons me, you lift me, drawing me near, for you too believe in the invisible that unites us.*

5. A Woven Ritual Garden

My obsession with that photograph of Hassiba's grand-mother, wearing around her head a white scarf embroi-dered with flowers, led me to search for a textile garden in Mogador. It would have to be something exceptional that Hassiba had never seen. I thought of the floral designs on traditional Berber capes, accompanied by intensely colored abstract figures. And also classic Persian carpets with archetypal flowers: little portable paradises. Both, no doubt, much too ordinary to suit Hassiba. I would have to find in Mogador a unique woven garden, perhaps from Persia, or south of the Sahara, or wherever.

I remembered a spectacular ritual costume from Chiapas, where myths are told with embroidered figures. Something like that must exist here. I thought that if there was an interesting cloth garden in Mogador, my friend Joseph would surely know of it, for in his shop under the Café Taros he sold, among other things, the most beauti-ful handmade fabrics of the region.

Not only did he not disappoint me, but he placed before my eyes one of the treasures from his personal col-lection, something few have had the privilege of seeing. From a trunk locked with five keys, he removed several pieces of woven fabric with similar textures. Together they made a single outfit, which, according to Joseph, has always been considered a treasure in Mogador. It had three parts: a skirt, a headdress, and a tunic, each embroidered with tiny flowers in three-dimensional stitching, with incredibly detailed precision.

It was brought to Mogador with the booty of an ancient pirate ship, and was handed down by generations of families living in the port for several centuries. It showed no signs of deterioration and was considered a magical object, full of *baraka*. It was known here as "Pizarro's Kaftan" because, according to legend, it was taken from him personally on the high sea by Mogadorian corsairs as he was returning from Peru with his treasures. Mogador, with its walled port, was a refuge for pirate ships, often those of the most famous buccaneers of Andalusi origin from Salé, who frequently ransacked Spanish vessels making ports of call in the Canary Islands during their journeys across the Atlantic. Piracy was a profitable, booming enterprise, financed by the city's merchants and nobles who competed with pirates from England and Portugal.

Those Mogadorians who had the fortune of crossing paths with Pizarro's ship and robbing him of what he in turn had stolen from Cuzco's golden temple, found themselves in the midst of one of the most terrible storms that had ever raged on that ocean. The danger of sinking was increased considerably by the tremendous weight of the gold they were carrying, and so in order to save it and survive, they decided to throw into the sea everything on the ship of lesser value, including food, cannon balls, chained prisoners, and even their own wounded. Two or three slaves of dazzling beauty were spared until the last moment, but eventually ended in the water.

When at last they had thrown overboard everything from their booty except the gold, to their surprise, the chest in which they would later discover "Pizarro's Kaftan," remained afloat, surrounded by a circle of tranquil water that gradually extended to the horizon. Something in that chest had quieted the storm and saved their lives (and their gold ingots). Overjoyed and amazed, they retrieved it from the water. They also managed to rescue the slaves, some monks who did not cease giving thanks to God, and a few nobles for whom they would demand ransom.

With curiosity and certain trepidation, they decided to see what was inside the miraculous chest. Many feared it held the remains of some Christian saint, which would have tested their faith. Others were certain that they would find a powerful amulet, more valuable than all the gold they carried. Or even a *jinn* could be inside, a genie waiting to satisfy all their desires. Still others shouted pleas not to open the chest under any circumstances because surely the storm had been captured inside and, if opened, would rise again to torment them, to take their lives (and their gold).

When all they took from the chest was a very intricate fabric of brilliant colors, with leaves and flowers embroidered in relief on the surface, they did not know exactly what they were seeing. They felt disappointed, but intrigued. One of the rescued monks took it upon himself to explain to them:

"What you see is a garden, perhaps the most ancient one of the New World. It was the spoils of war that the Inca rulers took from the descendants of a legendary civilization called the Chimu. The fabric is considered magical because it represents their paradise. They made a ritual tunic out of it for the priestesses to wear when they prayed at the top of the temple for the fertility of women and crops. According to legend, it can make rain fall in the desert. All the magical plants of the Chimu are reproduced on the fabric like sculptures of thread, as if the surface were the earth from which there rose a great variety of flowers and crops. All of them are recognizable: there is corn, and the coca flower, which dominates the design and whose leaves are used to make powerful brews, also the cotton flower, several tuberous plants, and many others. It is like one of our botanical treatises with beautiful laminates, but because those people did not have books, they told their stories in threads, in woven languages we can barely understand. On the surface, the plants are arranged in a geometric design with spirals ascending from the simple and visible to the hidden and invisible. Beneath that visible surface, there is another woven level where certain figures appear, perhaps their underworld gods, perhaps their dead. From their hearts sprouts each one of the flowers and plants. Perhaps they are the spirit of nature, its force emerging from a subterranean netherworld, from a hell where flowers do not burn but reproduce in the heat. Our elders, who have studied all of this, call them the demons of the garden. They believe they were the origin of lewdness and lust for those people."

The beauty and mystery of that vegetal costume took my breath away. And ever since that day, I cannot pass Joseph's shop without asking him to show it to me, to allow me to visit his woven garden, his paradise of threads warmed and nourished by a divine heart.

I wish to enter your heart guided by those threads. To go inside you from flower to roots. And return from death with you, donning the ironic smile that gives us life. To clothe ourselves with the magical garden and feel a luminous circle growing around us, capable of abating storms or unleashing them deep within us. I wish to roam in you from the visible to the invisible, from what I adore to what I have yet to discover, from one marvel to the next. I want to be the ritual gardener of those tattooed threads blossoming in you. To tend them and wander through them, to harvest their bouquets and powers. I want to be the priest devoted blindly to the botanical religion that every full moon you sow in me.

6. The Andalusi Palm Grove of Longing

Through the old Great East Gate, the main road led from Mogador to Marrakech, the city of palm groves. It stretched along both sides of the Muslim cemetery, as if bidding farewell to its dearly departed, then ran parallel to an aqueduct for several hundred yards before continuing on its own.

Inside the walls, the aqueduct nurtured a small palm grove, different from all others, and perfectly hidden from view of those approaching or leaving the city. The grove is not very tall, every inch having been calculated by an Andalusi *alarif*, a master artist who took into consideration the distance between each trunk, the curvature of its leaves, and even how much it would grow over the centuries. That grove is the Andalusi temple of Mogador, made only of palm trees and the ferns embedded in their trunks.

Among the Andalusi expelled from Spain were those who settled in Mogador hundreds of years before the new founding of the city in the eighteenth century and the construction of the walls that still stand today. One of them was a descendent of Ibn Hazm of Córdoba, who constructed a palace and this exceptional palm grove. It is not unique, however, because a half brother of his, who emigrated to America, erected another grove called *Palmar Chico*, a majestic imitation of its Mogadorian counterpart, whose ruins may still be admired in the heart of a jungle very near Costa Rica's Osa Peninsula. It just so happens that it was there that I was told some time ago about this one, which I had always believed to be mere legend. Today I found it here and learned that it is still cared for by its owners.

On the inside, it feels like being in a very sacred luminous space, full of light and shadows. From the outside, one marvels at the dark canopy it creates, as if it had a roof. Its ceiling of palm trees functions like latticework: invisible from the inside but quite opaque from the outside. The ferns provide a freshness that nearly takes away thirst without drinking. Serpents make their nests in the heart of the palm trees and slither out *en masse* every full moon to meet their destiny.

But what is most amazing about this palm grove is that its branches, as they cross, form perfect Moorish arches: two rows at different heights, evoking the arcade of the Great Mosque of Córdoba. They say the Andalusi architect was so homesick that he created an inverted reflection of his Cordoban mosque, whose columns are like perfect palm trees, and erected these palms that resemble living arches and columns.

The Great Mosque and its first arches also mirror another longing (according to the tale by the amazing and amazed Granadine author of *Córdoba of the Omeyas*). Imbued with nostalgia, Abd Al-Rahman imported from his native

Syria palm and pomegranate trees, which did not grow in Andalusia at that time, and planted them along the shores of the Guadalquivir, by the palace he built to model the one of his childhood. Many centuries later, in Mogador, the palm trees travel once again under the sign of desire. They reproduce not only a landscape but also a complete architecture, nature in stone, a paradoxical organic construction, like dreams, like desire.

Upon entering the Andalusi palm grove of Mogador, one understands that its architect not only longed for his lost mosque but also for the stirring yet serene feeling it provokes: a sensation of transcendence, of going beyond oneself, of touching the impossible and the perfect and the invisible with one's eyes and hands.

That is what I wish to be: stone and palm of your dreams. To erect here and there, wherever you step, the shadow that yearns for you. To sow in you, wherever you go, the palm of my hand balancing your serenity, which will be mine. I want to move beyond what can be seen. To discover in the deepest and freshest shadow of your shadows, the living temple where I adore you. My palm grows within your body, breathing and arching in your shadow. I am forever moved by the instant that unites us, and at your bidding, I touch the arch of longing within you.

7. The Garden of Arguments

On my daily quest for gardens to tell Hassiba, I met in the Jewish Quarter of Mogador, next to the silversmith market, a delightful man, known for his wisdom, who told me about a very strange garden that is the incarnation of all possible desires. After much insistence on my part, he explained where I could find that narrow strip of land that he called the "Garden of Arguments." He pointed toward a large building, overlooking the Dukala Gate, which had been a Dominican convent during the reign of the Portuguese, and then had served as barracks for more than a century.

Not long ago, the wishes of many citizens were granted when the military finally vacated the building. The people also managed to keep it from being turned into a hotel, a parking lot, or a shopping center. Eventually, it will be a community space for all Mogadorians to enjoy.

In the small developed area, there will be a museum of objects created and discarded in Mogador. And the court-yard, which occupies most of the land, will be converted into a public garden, something everyone agrees is much needed in Mogador.

In order to decide the garden's function and design, a commission of citizens was formed, comprised of experts from different professions and passions, two for each specialty. They worked for several months before presenting to the others what they considered to be the best plan for the garden. But something unexpected happened, which perhaps would not have occurred if the matter at hand had not concerned a garden, and if each of the delegates had not taken such a personal interest: not a single project received more than one vote. All of them clung to their own desires for the garden as if it were a matter of life and death. Obviously, the very idea of a garden awakens in the imagination desires and longings for paradise in which one invests not only the entire body, but also everything that gives meaning to life.

And so, the archeologists conducted excavations and decided that the garden should be an exhibit of the ancient seeds that they found there, leaving, of course, an immense hole in the ground to show how excavators work.

The historians insist that the garden include plants that the ancient herbalists of the city drew in their books and other documents preserved in the archives.

The biologists think a sampling of native and nonnative plants should be sown in alphabetical order, but one of the biologists believes they should follow the order of their Latin names, while the other proposes using their common names for planting the beds.

The painters, who are well-respected in the city, want a garden whose soil and plants are arranged according to their color. One of them has already found a mine with greenish-yellow dirt that matches certain plants perfectly. The other does not want to create an abstract painting, but rather an "installation" in which roses are grafted onto pomegranates, wigs placed on cacti, and trees planted with their leaves underground and their roots in the air. A conceptual garden presided over by a paper flower bearing a prosaic word: "transgression."

The conservationists want a garden of "plants in danger of extinction."

The ecologists envision trees as "green lungs" for the city.

The religious would like a retreat for prayer and contemplation.

The regionalists want an exhaustive representation of native plant life and are willing to pull up and burn all foreign species.

The anthropologists and ethnologists desire a garden of plants used by the diverse cultures of the city for cooking, medicine, clothing, and aesthetics.

The architects imagine a glass structure enclosing everything, supported by invisible hyper-technological columns at each end. The types of flowers are of little concern to them, provided some are made of concrete.

Faced with the difficult task of reaching an agreement, they decided to consult international commissions of experts in gardening. They arrived one by one, but instead of limiting themselves to their opinions about the proposed projects, they formulated their own desires as well.

The Japanese designed a very beautiful Zen garden of raked sand that reflected in great detail all the islands of

Mogador viewed from different angles: the coasts, its vegetation, the sea, and even the clouds.

The French envisioned and endorsed a garden that was perfectly geometric from every perspective. A garden so perfect it would make Versailles seem like an overgrown backyard. Its hedges would be pruned like walls, and its flowers and plants rotated almost daily, according to a two hundred year kaleidoscopic plan.

The English argued for a hill that was man-made but would not seem artificial, and a valley in which everything would appear entirely natural but be carefully studied and controlled.

The Italians proposed a baroque orientalist garden with grottos shaped like gigantic fauces and a thousand and one operatic fountains, one for each of Scheherazade's nights. And a labyrinth with no entry or exit.

The Mexican specialists decided to create on the sea and just inside the city walls some very fertile floating islands, connected by canals, which would allow them to flood the city and then dry it out with each change in government.

The Brazilians would produce a theatrical representation of Amazonian vegetation, with a cardboard jungle, flying birds, and the destruction of the rainforest by commercial loggers, to be presented each day at sunrise and sunset.

The Peruvians drew up a flawless plan that consisted of bringing to Mogador, from the most florid countries of the northern Mediterranean, millions and millions of boatloads of fertile soil. Just as the ancient Quechuas had done in the Sacred Valley, they would pile all that dirt onto terraces, erected in the desert as if they were mountains. And then, as can be seen in Lima, enormous concrete water basins would be placed on posts, leaving future archeologists to wonder if the people were ritual worshipers of cisterns.

The Venezuelans planned to mix vegetation and cement, placing automobiles in the garden and setting up shops of splendid exotic plants on every corner.

The debate goes on, even as new commissions of specialists are summoned with the hope that a resolution can finally be made for this future garden, the object of so many fantasies: the ideal garden, the essential garden, abounding, for the moment, with those exotic flowers of reason that their gardeners call arguments.

Like this, Hassiba, I sow in the garden that we conceive each day my passion and the meaning of my life. But I do not wish to plan beyond the first step I take. If your desires change, each day I will invent a new dream for your essential gardens and begin to labor in each one, even if you ask me to take another path right away. I want to dream incessantly that I may reach you through your dreams, touch you in them, and shed mine for yours.

8. The Garden of Traveling Cacti

A Canadian writer named Scott Symons took a vacation to Mogador in the mid-seventies and decided to stay there forever. He has a house and a garden on the outskirts of the city. Not long ago, he expressed his desire to donate his garden to the city. For more than twenty-five years, he has collected cacti, and has an immense variety of them, the majority of them Mexican. He got them from a couple of Canadian artists who have lived in a semi-arid zone of Mexico since the forties: the photographer Reva Brooks and her husband, the painter and musician Leonard Brooks. Together with Sterling Dickinson, and Dotty Vidargas and her husband, the Brookses have worked diligently to preserve the integrity and beauty of the city of San Miguel de Allende. They were also responsible for the "cactus bridge" to Mogador that made it possible to create the Mexican garden of the walled city.

Like all gardens, this one expresses the extravagant desires that govern the spirit of those who create and cultivate them. Our transplanted gardener wished to bring to Mogador, to the desert's edge, succulent plants that did not grow in that desert. Not only did he want to add new varieties to the place, but he wished, as he told me when he invited me there, "to make this landscape more faithful to itself."

There is something evangelical about his attitude, like

the sects who study the Bible and argue over who reads and interprets most faithfully the "holy word." It seems strange that he wanted to make Mogador more faithful to itself by introducing a part of Mexican nature to the heart of this land, but as Scott used to say, "the desert spreads to the desert."

As if I could transplant myself with all my thorns and sand, and take root so naturally in your fertile Saharian body.

I think about the hundreds of cacti that have traveled for-tuitously and perhaps secretly. It no longer matters where they came from. They live in Mogador and belong there now, and nowhere else.

As I wish to be yours and nothing else matters.

I remember the land I saw as a boy in the Sonoran Desert, and suddenly it occurs to me that my journey to the Sahara has awakened in my memory a part of that child-hood, and it lives again precisely because I am here.

Day and night images of that distant time come back to me, visions that for so many years I did not know I had forgotten. What is reborn in the memory of those cacti that are so happy in Mogador?

What is reborn in the depths of my skin when I kiss you? I want your body to flow and flower in mine, remembering or reinventing your inner garden that unites us. I want the desert of your body to identify with mine through the mystery of their nomadic plants.

Perhaps these cacti are like those aquatic Mexican *axolotls* that a scientist brought to Paris in the nineteenth century to study them in the *Jardin des Plantes.* The water there had so much calcium that they climbed out of their aquarium and became what they had the potential of being: amphibian salamanders. In no time at all, they developed the capacity for breathing and hearing and could leave the water and walk on what before they had used to swim.

I wish to become that impossible being that dwells within the boundaries of your skin and is reborn there, to be the air caressing your naked body, the voices that persuade you effortlessly. I will be one of those voices that searches for you, like a tree whose airy roots dive into the dew to enter the earth. I will be the voice that desires you, entering and leaving you like the amphibian that devours and contemplates you.

9. The Garden of Flowers and their Echoes

On one of the hills that surround Mogador to the north-west, a woman planted flowers called "Slaves of the Rainbow." Their blossoms have lustrous petals that create visions rivaling the most beautiful ones ever experienced by mystics of any religion. Unfortunately, the flowers are doomed to perish after blooming only one day. If some-one picks their leaves and withered petals at night, the same plant flowers again the next day with blossoms of a different color. People begin to sow the flowers with great enthusiasm, but soon abandon them, exhausted by all the attention they require, thus bringing about the demise of the entire plant. A woman named Lalla planted a hillside with more than a hundred yards of those flowers, spacing them very close together like a tapestry of dazzling hues, and then decided to become their slave.

"I will be just another slave of the rainbow," Lalla declares, playing with the name of the flowers to deride those who criticize her incessant labor. Each day she dons a different color to harmonize with her dazzling field.

And indeed it is worth stopping along the road to admire that flowering hillside. Now there is a photogra-pher who records the graphic history of the changes. He hangs the photos on a wall in the plaza of Mogador, cre-ating a strange painting of varying colors: a second garden that also changes each day.

Because the light fades the colors of the photographs, a painter from Mogador decided to reproduce them on another wall of the plaza with brushes and paints resistant to light, wind, salt, and humidity. All of us in Mogador pass by there several times a day, expressing our opinions about this or that detail on the walls. Other photographers spend their time recording the daily progress of the photographer and painter.

Some citizens thought that neither the painter nor the photographer were faithful to the beauty of the hillside and the emotions kindled by its rainbow flowers. So poets answered the call and gather weekly in the plaza to put on an arousing show of verbal flowers that evoke the essence of the real ones. Now rival and allied groups have formed, the press has intervened, and intrigues abound and flourish.

Much to the children's delight, a baker has debuted a kaleidoscopic pastry, naming it "Rainbow Pie." In the restaurants of the port, one may order either the traditional *bastila* filled with pigeon or chicken, the new seafood variation, or the latest version made of rainbow flowers.

The musicians want their piece of the pie and compose an unending number of popular songs that have become a new genre of Mogadorian music: rainbow blues. Even the *Gnawa* musicians have assimilated them into their ritual invocation of spirits.

Lalla has no time to discover all that her garden has

unleashed, although there is always someone who goes and tells her, in lavish detail, what is said about her and her flowers. These rumors, and what I write now, form one more link in the chain of echoes released by these flowers that enslave all of us in Mogador. Together they form what is known as a Rainbow Flower culture, and in a broader sense, a symbolic cultivation of that blossoming.

You are my flowering hillside and with my hands I want to unleash my adoration for you. I will never cease to cover you with caresses. I will cultivate the infinite smiles on all the mouths of your body I wish to photograph them, paint them, bite them, write them, sing them, and whisper them in your ear, as if you did not know that it is for them that I live. I want you to let me tend your hills, shedding my skin each day to harmonize with your variations, with your echoes.

THIRD SPIRAL
GARDENS IN AN INSTANT

Nine Bonsai

I am a plant with no name
in the swift currents
of your stream.
Chiun

1.
From afar I smell
magnolias in your womb
unraveling me.

2.
From all sides
my delirious frogs
leap into your pond.

3.
I am that stubborn water
seeking day and night
all your roots.

4.
Between your thighs
toward your dew-lipped flower
my insects crawl.

5.
The fervent leaves
chant your name
my wind follows ablaze.

6.
Your ravenous flower
traps me in flight
dawn breaks within.

7.
Avidly your black sun
devours me
I cry out inflamed.

8.
Surrender all secrets
your spring whispers
surrender to me now.

9.
The bee buzzes
round your legs
incited by your lips.

Fourth Spiral
Intimate and Minimal Gardens

I. The Most Intimate Garden

The poet Henri Michaux, who traveled incessantly, visited Mogador and bought an apple there. He does not say exactly where. But that night, in his hotel (we presume he was traveling alone this time), he wrote about his intimate desire for an orchard or fruit garden, later including it in his work *Au pays de la magie*:

> "I place an apple on the table. Then I enter the apple. What marvelous tranquility!"

Gaston Bachelard quotes him and analyzes this idea throughout an entire chapter of his book on poetic imagination and its relationship to earth and our longing for intimacy. He compares it repeatedly to the sensation that Gustave Flaubert professes toward all the things of this world that captivate him:

> "When I gaze long enough upon a stone, animal or painting, I feel that I enter them."

Bachelard says that, although it may seem contradictory, Michaux's garden is more complete because it is so minuscule. The philosopher is certain that in the poetic contemplation of matter, a paradox inevitably arises: the interior of a small object is always larger and more poignant than an immense one.

After pondering Michaux's apple, I feel the urge to run to the market of Mogador and buy an apple like his to see if I too can enter it. Zen meditation, French style, with food.

But more than anything else, I think obsessively about you. Returning to my memory and to my thirst for desire is that day I awoke to find you naked, by my side, with your head at the other end of the bed. The sheets nearly covered you, except for your sex, which I admired from behind while it rested like a tantalizing fruit, perfectly framed by the roundest form of your body, appearing, from that angle, tiny like the core of half an apple. That comparison mesmerized me completely.

I imagined you were my apple, my orchard of tranquility, my most intimate garden. And I wanted to be deep inside you, happy like Michaux in his tiny fortuitous orchard in Mogador.

2. The Minimal Garden of Stones in the Wind

It is a very small garden on the rooftop of one of the houses overlooking the ramparts of Mogador, very near the fortress of the Sqala, where the wind blows with greatest force. A man who was once gardener to the king, and knew all there was to know about growing plants, decided after retiring to create a garden in his house. Actually, a garden of stones.

He selected very beautiful river stones, which are rare in Mogador, about the size of a large open hand. He bore a hole through the center, as if to make a necklace out of them, and inserted into each one a slender metal rod the size of a little girl's finger. Each rod, approximately two feet long, including the stone on the end, was imbedded into the roof of his house and exposed to the wind.

The distance between each stone is enough for the wind to move them so that they strike each other, producing strange music. It is like a field of fragile flowers stirred by the wind. And because in Mogador the only thing that is never lacking is the wind, the flowers move night and day. Of course they sing a different tune depending on the wind that pushes them, the humidity and salt in the air, or the intensity of the sun, which is capable of suspending all movement.

A rare sensation emanates from this garden: the fragility of a flower in a material known to be hard. A tranquility that awakens the desire to continue contemplating it.

"I love to listen to my garden," says the retired gardener, who has sown and tended more plants than anyone in the kingdom. I ask if he misses his royal gardens.

"Even the king would envy me my garden of stones in the wind. It is the most beautiful one that can be found in the world."

Like him, I wish to ride the wind with my dreams and create the unexpected in your body. Can you imagine that I sow in you a passion that resounds whenever I draw near?

3. The Garden of Clouds

More than the renowned passion of the Mogadorian gardeners for fountains, more than their ability to tune them subtly like musical instruments, more than the spectacular beauty of their garden pools, and their streams and channels, more than the zealous and indispensable cult of water in the desert, all of us are amazed by the story of a gardener from Mogador who decided to cultivate water and harvest it, not from wells in the earth, but from the clouds themselves.

Inspired by a strange garden in Chile's Atacama Desert, he decided to erect a tower that would reach the clouds. At first people thought he was insane when he ordered the weavers of fishing nets in the port to make him a very special one with inverted triangles. When they asked in what boat he would use it, he said it was not for catching fish but for trapping clouds. No one could believe him. He was either foolish or mocking all of them with sarcasm. Nevertheless, he meant every word he said.

He owned some land on a coastal area of the Sahara, where it was impossible to grow anything. There was no water, and seawater was of no use. In a journal dedicated to unusual phenomenon, he read the story of a Chilean man who had a garden in Chugungo, a town where water was scarce. The water finally ran out and the gardener did not know what to do to keep his garden from dying, as well as everything else planted in the town. The Chilean explains that the village sits on a strip of the desert, by the sea, with a gigantic cliff behind it that is so tall its summit blends with the clouds rolling in from the sea.

At the cliff's edge, he erected a net of inverted triangles that captured the moisture from the clouds, in the form of dew, which saturated each strand. As the dew condensed, it trickled toward the lowest point of each triangle, which in turn, collected the water from those above.

The end product was more than sixty thousand quarts of water daily for a town that had been condemned to die from drought. What impresses me most is that this gardener had invented a system for harvesting or fishing water because his garden was going to die if he did not find a solution. His personal need, and that of the town, would have been enough motivation, but that was not the case. In that interview, he recognizes that perhaps he would not have been able to come up with this idea had the life of his garden not been at stake. Gardeners, like all collectors, are capable of the most extraordinary actions. They often value the life of their plants over their own.

They speak of the nebulous gardener of Mogador as a madman clinging to a ridiculously high ladder, casting his fisherman's net toward the first cloud that passes by, if some day one ever will. Meanwhile, he constructs his tower as high as he can, considering he has no cliff at his disposal. The higher he climbs, the more he realizes that very few clouds ever cross his desert. Yet he perseveres, with nets on his back, climbing toward the sky in search of water for his garden, like a desperate lover in manic pursuit of his beloved's gaze.

That is how I feel as I pursue you, erecting a tower toward the sky, pausing and enjoying each instant as I reach your dewy point, which always, gently, arouses me.

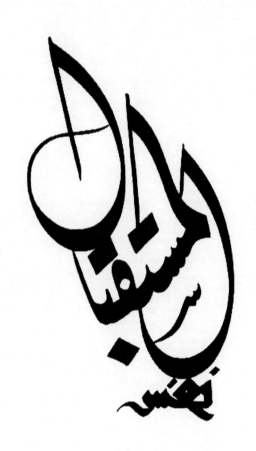

4. The Garden of No Return

Although the architect León R. Zahar states that the famous and enigmatic Blue Palace, Al Azrak, was located somewhere between Samarkand and Baghdad, documents found in Mogador indicate otherwise. Alonso Páez, a rebel from the ill-fated 1403-1405 expedition of Ruy González de Clavijo, Spanish ambassador to Samarkand and Bujara, attests in a letter to another location that is no less problematic.

Alonso Páez felt obliged to leave his traveling companions for having expressed opinions about a fundamental matter that differed radically from those of his commander, his Excellency, the ambassador. Páez insisted that the water from a spring near their camp was pure and drinkable. The crystal transparency of the pond, and the appearance of its golden reflections shimmering in the sun, had convinced him of it. Superficial reasons, according to his commander, whose experience in diplomacy had taught him to question systematically all that glittered.

But Páez had already appeased his thirst with that splendor and deep transparency. With that conviction on the tip of his tongue, he rebelled openly against his commander, drank that water with abandon, and encouraged his fellow companions to unite with him in that delectable pleasure of savoring the truth.

In the diaries of Ruy González de Clavijo, that incident concludes with the illness and delirium of Alonso Páez, and the five who joined him, in what the chronicler calls, not without irony: "The extinct rebellion of the dry tongue, drowned in the same insidiously putrid water that had been the object of his desire and the reason for his uprising."

It is in one of his letters to an Andalusian maiden, who in those years perturbed him more than his fever, that Páez narrates his chance discovery of the Blue Palace and its gardens. In the grips of fever, he remembers that they carried him on a stretcher at the rear of the expedition, and as they drew near the city of Samarkand, they set up camp on a hill, where they received the order of the sultan to approach a certain gate in the wall, leaving the sick men behind. It was then that he decided to embark, with the rebels of the dry tongue, on a painstaking return to the last city they had come across.

This band of retreating invalids, along with a pair of guards and a few women who accompanied them, lost their way. The guide became infected, no one is certain how, although the likely source may have been a relentless exchange of kisses.

After some time (no one knows how many days because by then the group could not count with any certainty the suns that had risen and set), they came to the region of dunes, which they would later learn, surround the walled city of Mogador.

Before discovering this, they saw off in the distance a shimmering blue that riveted their pupils. And they thought that there was truth to the legend (documented by Alberto Manguel and Gianni Guadalupi in their *Dictionary of Imaginary Places*) about the town of Abaton and its Blue Palace: a town without a definite location, which materializes when invoked by desire, and lives to be desired. Those travelers who search earnestly for her fail, while many others have seen her rise suddenly above the horizon, without having summoned her. They come to need her, and in the end, cannot live without her.

"Like all that surrounds Mogador, this is the palace of desire," Páez would write later, "and as such it obeys the capricious laws of the desirable: it wrenches from us what we foolishly long for, and unexpectedly hands us what we did not know we truly needed, something perfectly tuned to our bodies."

Another palace can only be seen from a distance by those in love, as if that condition sharpened their vision, so I was told at the gates of Mogador by Claire, wife of the poet Jamal Eddine Bencheikh, editor and translator, along with André Miquel, of the most beautiful version of *One Thousand and One Arabian Nights.*

According to Sir Thomas Bullfinch, who three centuries later would become the great western chronicler of Abaton, the blue splendor of the palace is accompanied in the distance by the music of tambourines and strings, which reaches the ears of the traveler, never to be forgotten. Scents arrive in waves, blending overly sweet smells with those of unfamiliar flowers, aromas that provoke and possess.

Páez describes in detail, albeit hastily, his arrival to the palace, concentrating primarily on the gardens. This complements the meticulous, yet evocative description provided by León R. Zahar, who, on the contrary, passes quickly through the gardens and lingers in the palace. Both touch the captivating essence of that place that some still refuse to believe exists.

"For several days we wondered if we were alive or already in paradise, because once we entered the gardens of the Blue Palace, there was no possible reason for us to leave them. They seemed to be contained within an inner patio, within four walls of the Palace, a *ryad*, we were told. But it was merely an illusion because no angle offered a complete view of that alleged enclosure. After going down a few terraces, we came to one of the possible centers of the blue garden, to a fountain buried in the ground, where four streams converged, reminding us of the four legendary rivers of Eden. Trees were placed below the terraces, creating orchards planted in nearly indecipherable geometric patterns. After crossing several terraces, we realized we had walked more than the length of the palace, and that the garden, rather than being contained within, encompassed it.

"The extraordinary architecture of its tiles was yet another flower of paradise. Blue flowers reigned by day, and the swarming bees seemed like a sea above the trees. These flowers, which mirrored the tiles, closed at night, and in the moonlight a swell of white flowers opened like a foaming wave."

"The fountains sung, as in all the Arabic gardens we have visited on this journey, but here their song seemed to repeat the names of the lovers who, according to a legend I was told, will never again leave these paths. And if my name, Alonso Páez, were not engraved forever in the aqua voice of this garden of the Blue Palace, with pleasure I would have returned to see you."

Deep in fever, lost in my thirst for you, I long to see you rise above the horizon, becoming forever indispensable. To enter that part of you whose existence others cannot conceive because they do not know the depth and powers of your inner gardens, those that enclose and embrace me, yet seem minute enough to devour. I want my name to remain forever engraved in your fountain so that I may never leave your dominions.

5. The Garden of Voices

In an ancient corner of Mogador, city of countless immi-grations, of blood and tongues and dreams that intersect in an infinite arabesque, there once was a small but very vibrant Chinatown whose interior gardens were not created with plants but stones. According to legend, those strange rocks had been brought by sea from distant countries where silk was sold. Besides their beauty, they had the natural gift of covering themselves with a spongy red moss that spread quickly. That is why in the city they used to say that the humidity there made the stones grow until they touched the sky, where only the clouds could soothe them.

In that same legendary corner of Mogador, very near the walls, between the East Gate and the sea, there is a gar-den of crickets who sing all day long for their blind gardener. Those who visit it in the morning, may see the gardener shredding intently every plant he can find, including the most beautiful and rare. That always upsets those who watch him for the first time, unaware that in this garden there are no leaves or flowers except for those torn and placed in the small cages by that man as food for his crickets.

The gardener knows which plants each tiny creature loves to eat and which can lower or raise its pitch. He clas-sifies and names the flowers for their digestive values, that is, for the range of sounds they will help to produce once digested, as if the only or principle reason for being of each flower was to transform itself into a beautiful cricket song. "The flower is to the song what the caterpillar is to the butterfly. Astonishing metamorphosis," he would tell his visitors.

We are also intrigued by the boxes made of wood, ivory, or bone, where he keeps his crickets. Some are quite simple, but no less beautiful, with straw bars and sliding doors over small wooden tongues. They hang from the trees like fruits that sing when someone draws near. Others are tiny statues. The gardener himself has adorned them with fine woods and inscribed in calligraphy the name he gives each cricket, a name originating from the range of sounds it emits. He also carves a sign that describes their place in the garden of voices.

Before him, his father did this, and his grandfather, and the father of his grandfather. One hundred years ago there were twenty decorative cages tended by his great-grandfather like an exquisite orchard. His son multiplied the orchard by five, and the grandson by ten. And so this gardener inherited a thousand cages and a small fortune to maintain them, plus the family tradition refined by three generations before him, not counting the centuries this art was cultivated in China. Over twenty-five years this man has made the garden grow and now nearly three thousand cages form labyrinthine paths, a web very similar to that created by the streets of the city. Those incapable of orienting themselves by the chirping run the risk of losing themselves forever in this garden. Shouts for help would be useless, just one more among many.

There are many things, besides food, that may alter the chanting of the crickets, and one of them is invisible and powerful: desire. The gardener knows that placing certain cages next to others will lead to enthusiastic courtship calls throughout the night. And he knows that if he separates them, little by little a deep sorrowful tone dominates that song. Distance is an imaginary chord of longing that he fine tunes continuously.

The love song of these creatures is so poignant and resolute that for a very long time the poets of Mogador and its surroundings have compared it to that intuitive passion one body has for another. Ibn Hazm says that when two lovers look at each other from a distance "all the crickets of their bodies tingle hungrily."

Aziz Al-Gazali writes that in Mogador the crickets search for the warmth of fire, which is why they stay in kitchens, near the community bread ovens, or by the cauldrons of the public steam baths, the *hammans*, where often they are displayed as an emblem, carved in the entrance. The story is also told that in the house of a woman named Fatma, "who saw her senses flower suddenly in the surprising light of desire; crickets had nestled beneath her bed and sang like springtime and summer, even on the rawest days of winter."

Everyone in Mogador seems to agree that crickets sing differently during each season of the year, and are even capable of announcing their arrival. Well trained, they can measure precisely the temperature of the day. This gardener always goes to extremes and has raised a type of cricket that can measure the temperature of the body. It is quite small and its voice is faint and low but vibrates forcefully. This species is called "the smile of the moon." Some have discovered that it begins singing when the desire between two people increases, and naturally their body heat as well. Some carry the crickets on their romantic encounters, hidden in their clothes, very close to the skin, so they may feel the vibration of their song rather than hear it.

That is why Ibn Hazm, in a book that follows his poetic manual of love, *The Necklace of the Dove*, includes a chapter in which he instructs the suitor to search with patience and prolonged expectation among the thousand folds of the beloved's garments for those denouncing crickets, and then advises the lover to continue searching the folds of his mistress's naked body as if he could find in them a thousand "smiles of the moon."

In this garden of Mogador, before the sun rises, when a veil of dew falls gently over the cages and deposits inside them several thick drops, the crickets can be heard drinking. Their whistles trickle, their joy gurgles. If they drink too much before the sun rises, a strange involuntary vibration rises from them, as if they were shivering from cold.

Some afternoons when the wind is still, the blind gardener searches for the clouds of mosquitos that gather on the southern end of the beach just as the sun sets. He lets them bite him until, swollen with blood, they can no longer fly, and he captures them easily to offer as a delicacy to some of his crickets, particularly those dark obese ones that sing as they eat, with deep notes that ring out their happiness like tolling bells.

The gardener recognizes each one by its sounds. He knows that science has developed several efficient methods for classifying them, but he only cares to distinguish them by their voices, which he does with remarkable precision. He has come to identify with certainty 2633 different types of sounds. He had to subtract four from his list this year when he realized that the crickets did not make them, but he himself, or rather his body, while walking quickly, breathing heavily on hot days, sighing contently while listening to his creatures, or digesting with difficulty those leaves and flowers that his animals left untouched and he did not wish to waste.

When night falls, a scribe enters the garden cautiously to offer his services, should the gardener wish to record new sounds. His list grows and he continually refines each description. So, for example, next to *Echoes of drops over fire: sound 1327*, reads the description: "Like saliva between the teeth; like a sudden longing to drink. This repeats itself in intervals of ten drops, each alike."

But the gardener is never satisfied with those transcriptions in words and so he has invented a type of score composed of small river stones of different shapes that he places on a long table. He knows very well that his arrangement of pebbles would undoubtedly be considered a pile of rubble by others, but that transcription, which only he understands, is also a tactile map of the sounds of his garden. At night, he catches himself humming it out loud. On more than one occasion, his own chanting of the map has led him to shift the cages and thus modify the composition of his unusual pebble bed.

Moved by the intensity of certain voices in his garden, and brimming with pride for his role in producing them, some of the sounds that he discovered appear on the list bearing his own name. They are his creatures. And the stories he likes to tell about each cage, about how he trapped or was able to incubate each insect, about the life and habits of his little beasts, could enthrall whoever had the good fortune to hear them, as if *The Canterbury Tales*, or those of the *Decameron*, or *One Thousand and One Arabian Nights* were inspired by this garden of crickets.

He has learned to control many of those hundreds of insect sounds. He can make them reproduce: in a way he is capable of sowing them. He experiences his greatest happiness when he hears them blossom and mature.

At times even what others see and what he only touches becomes a sound for this blind man, if it is truly amazing. That happens in different ways but especially with a creature that came to Mogador by boat from a walled city of Guinea. It is a strange type of beautiful grasshopper that reigns pretentiously over his garden: its wings, more beautiful and shimmering than a *Morpho* butterfly, are twice the size of its immense body. They are green and yellow and purple. And the chirping of this cricket unfolds that coloring in a way that only the gardener hears.

For him, blind from birth, like his father and grandfather, space does not exist if it does not produce sounds. The very idea of a silent garden is something he cannot imagine. Voices sprout around him, they flower, grow orchards, create an enveloping haven, sensations of distance and intimacy, of depth and resounding perspective, of inaccessible beauty, and naturally, of desire.

Perhaps that is why some say that the gardener is not blind, but merely closes his eyes most of the day to reproduce the sensation of walking among voices sown, blossoming, and gathered.

I always recall that garden whenever you touch me with closed eyes and your breathing adjusts to mine. When at night my name intertwines indecipherably with yours. When we no longer know what we tell each other, and tenderness flows in long vowels, sighs, moans, and hoarse whispers. When I search in you, even in the folds of your dreams, the most ephemeral smiles of the moon. When I think of you and listen to you, my garden of voices.

6. The Cannibal Garden

The strangest *ryad* of Mogador is completely hidden from view and can only be entered through a narrow door at the back of a butcher shop. It smells like raw meat and the excrement of bats. For three generations, a family of butchers has cultivated cannibal plants there. A primitive kind of ficus, these trees slowly encircle others, dehydrating, rotting, and finally killing them. Their seeds are so hard that for them to open and germinate, they must first absorb the gastric juices of certain bats that adore their fruits so much that they are willing to fight to the death for them.

Other trees, with a long life-span, must be burned in the forest for their seeds to open and reproduce, but for this ficus strangler, hungry warrior bats suffice.

When one of the bats wins the battle, it chokes down the entire fruit, even its large and bitter seed. The bat expels it in his excrement on the branch of the tree, where he had taken refuge to calmly devour his prize. Fertilized there, the seed is able to open and germinate. Into the air it thrusts a shoot that latches onto the trunk of its host tree and slowly begins its descent, circling the trunk and covering it until it reaches the ground.

When the ficus strangler finally claws its roots into the earth, the tree that shelters it is doomed to certain death.

In the rain forest of Monte Verde in Costa Rica, I saw

a ficus that had stood hollow for a long time. The thick tree it had strangled was nothing more than forgotten sawdust. The invader had taken its shape, but its veins never completely covered the body of its victim. Its trunk was like a flawed copy of the other tree, but its exterior was so full of holes that I could peer into its inner void, a detail that made it all the more disturbing and fascinating. Children, veritable lovers of the terrifying, used it as a ladder to climb more than sixty feet to the tree tops, that region of the rain forest where everything teems with life.

The head butcher of Mogador loves to observe how one plant suffocates another in his cannibal *ryad*, where a new plant will always emerge to do the same to its predecessor. The bats are also happy in this garden, their favorite *ryad*.

You know that I wish to be like those bats and eat your fruits. And if need be, I will fight for them. You know that I want to be those ravenous branches that strangle and encircle you, devouring you with tenderness. But I also wish you to be those branches, climbing my trunk. You know that my desire for you takes my breath away and transforms me into the ladder I blissfully mount to reach you.

7. The Garden of Winds

These were very great forces increasing . . .
error and wonder prospered,
and the green locust of sophistry;
virulences of the spirit at the edge of salt flats
and the freshness of erotism at the entrances to forests.
Saint-John Perse

Beware of women who blow
on the knots of a string.
They have entangled your destiny.
Moroccan Proverb

It was the hour in Mogador when lovers rouse. The nine winds of the morning wrap them, as they do everyone and everything, in another cloak of darkness, an invisible prolongation of night. And in that languid river of tangled winds, the lovers bathe their desires once again. There, floating in time, without stirring, they caress each other.

That is what the storyteller, the *halaiki* says, and everyone in the city swears that we should believe him. "Sometimes he reveals to us what will happen tomorrow, other times he reminds us of what we saw when we first came to the city, or what happened to us yesterday." The *halaiki* speaks of winds, of loves, of himself, of all of us:

All the travelers who awaken in Mogador at dawn can see how nine winds always greet the rising sun:

- From the sand that slips beneath the closed doors, we know the eastern dunes are launching their daily attack on the city, mounting an early morning current known as The Easterner.

- From the grains of salt hurled against the walls, a thousand times at the same hour, by dark and balmy southern gusts, we know aurora draws near.

- From the slight creaking of the ceilings, braced with sensitive and capricious timber, we know the deep chill of the night is preparing its departure.

- From the anxious fluttering of the seagulls (between wind and sea, spattered with foam) we know the fish in the bay are now visible to them: the distant sun, behind the arched horizon, plunges into the sea far away and illuminates it here, from below, shortly before dawn.

• From the water in the fountains that splash away the last traces of the moon, we also know that morning is nigh.

• From the pomegranates, whose crowns bow to the wind and skins burst, still clinging to the tree, exposing the throng of blushing suns they bear within.

• From the fleshy leaves (poets describe as "shaped like a woman's lips kissing the wind") of the flower called the Mogadorian Impatiens, which begins to turn toward the sun long before it shows its golden mane.

• From the kaftans, freshly washed, starched and hung on the rooftops, that dance in the wind as they await the sun, as if remembering the music, the anticipation, the compliment, perhaps the embrace that made their mistresses perspire.

• From the growing kicks of infants who, after

three months in their mother's wombs, awaken at that very hour to listen, through the tight dome of skin shielding them, to the chorus of winds that intertwine, forming concentric circles in that belly, like those whirling above all the tiled cupolas of the city.

There are those who have given names to what cannot be seen here. The morning winds of Mogador, which I just described, are known by sailors as the Garden of Winds. The pirates used them to protect their territory. Only the buccaneers of Mogador could navigate the invisible paths that would allow them to enter and leave the port, leading their enemies to believe that they had sown them. The exotic flowers, the trees, the fruits of this Garden of Winds are called: The Easterner, The Black One, The Whiner, The Wing of the Seagull or The Wing of Foam, The Envy of the Moon, The King of Pomegranates, The Impatient Mouth, The Great Dance or The Restless Seduction, and The Wind of the Cupolas. To unleash them, one must learn to recognize them. They converge in the city, running through its streets and between the legs and ears of its residents, gathering finally in that

primal wind, so eloquent and subtle, known as
The Morning Knot, or The Pregnant Spiral, or
simply The Spiral of Desires. And that is where
all the stories of Mogador worth telling begin.
This is where I begin my work, once I see and
hear on the skin of my tambourine the jingling
coins released by your hands.

All this was declared, with cries and precise gestures, by the
most famous ritual storyteller of the Main Plaza of
Mogador, the Plaza of the Snail, as he seduced his faithful and curious audience, always happy to listen to him.

*I want to be all the winds that lie in wait for you, that cling to you,
that run even through your veins. The winds that dry your clothes and
cool your body. I want to be the wind of your voice, of your soul.*

8. The Garden of Fire

It smells of smoke and its pleasure has no bounds, as if it were the perfume of a rare flower, new to his garden, acquired with infinite patience. This gardener discovered many years ago, during a fire in the forest, that roots continue to burn beneath the ground long after the flames are supposedly extinguished. It was then that he decided to cultivate a garden of highly flammable roots, controlling their subterranean fire beds with buried channels of water in such a way that, like bouquets of fire flowers, the flames sprout to the surface, igniting the thicket or trees that he selects.

He walks in his garden of underground fires, sensing through his skin the heat that flows slowly beneath the ground. He designs routes and controls them, irrigating here and there the banks of his channels. And when at last the blazing flower opens where he wishes, he recognizes in the burning plant the ephemeral perfumed blossom of his ardent fancy.

The network of roots, which he cannot see, adds a great number of unforeseen fires to his harvest. Heat runs through unsuspected beds, surprising him when it breaks out where he least expects it. Then the beauty of his flowers becomes convulsive, brutal. A sudden elation comes over the gardener at that moment, and the gleam of the flames in his eyes is kindled by the combustion in his mind.

When the sun kisses the horizon, the gardener sometimes imagines that he planted that fire in the sky, that an unforeseen and invisible aerial root guides his fire to the clouds, converting them into flickers, embers, and finally charcoal.

He discovered that the night is just that, endless coal. And that the stars are tiny souvenirs of fire embedded in the great carbon vault. Fossilized flowers. Then it dawns on him that it takes millions of years and millions of gardeners to tend his garden so that the blazing flowers he grows may shine each night on their own. Meanwhile, when darkness covers everything, the gardener draws, with radiant flowers from his garden, a celestial map, a geometry of shooting stars. At first he wanted to mirror the sky exactly, but later he felt compelled to sketch his own constellations.

Some come at night to read their destiny, or that of their loved ones, in the stellar drawing of this fiery field. And the curator of the Great Underground Library of Mogador proposes that more than a few revolutions, what he calls "fire in the human mind," began as one of the glimmering flowers in this garden, and likewise, the roots of uprisings in China, Iran, or Patagonia extend back to this place.

Whenever the gardener sows, waters, and illuminates, he knows he is planting an unexpected spark in the world, that the beauty of his garden shakes empires, perhaps even burns stars in the firmament, dries rivers on other continents, demolishes skyscrapers in flames, and beheads kings.

There are also those who believe that each sudden flare in this garden corresponds to a heartbreaking passion. That neither Romeo nor Juliet, neither Abelard nor Heloise escaped the power of these roots, which in a mysterious but infallible manner, reach all the way to the heart of certain people.

The other day, the gardener was walking down the street and noticed that two strangers, a man and a woman, were staring at each other with desiring eyes. There were simultaneous sparks in their pupils, and judging from their intensity, and the fact that not all plants burn the same way, the gardener knew in what part of his garden that fiery passion had originated. So he ran to the southern orchard of dry palm trees to observe from his terrace the splendor of that spontaneous blossoming. And contemplating his garden, he knew in what moment the desire between that couple overflowed, how long they made love, and when their passion had extinguished.

I think about this garden when I feel on your skin the warmth surging through your veins, when you slowly and intently cross the few inches that separate us, as if you came from very far away. When your entire body guides me to the most intense heat within you, which little by little consumes me between your legs, those two great flames that, like an uncontrollable fire kindled by the wind, seize me, binding me to you.

I think about the happiness of this gardener when time and time again the joy of mutual possession burns in your eyes, when your mouth barely emits a crackle, the sound of a sudden flare. When you embrace me and you are embers, when you kiss me and you are that one who lets your entire body be filled with roots of fire, keeping alive forever the promise of a radiant flower that ignites us.

9. The Solar Flower

It was the hour in Mogador when lovers rouse. Their dreams blend with the sounds they hear. I dreamed I was sailing, or perhaps I really was sailing toward Mogador. I was returning from the Purpurine Islands, which seem to float in front of the port, where I had gone in search of new gardens. I thought obsessively about the charge that I had been given by Aisha, who read the cards for me when I consulted her about my quest for gardens for Hassiba.

"Take leave of yourself and return when you are another. Before long, you will have regained your paradise. Become a voice, an echo repeated nine times. Nine like the winding spiral that never ends and turns in on itself."

After coming ashore, I was amazed to hear an *halaiki* telling, in the Open Plaza of the Port, a story very similar to mine, as if I myself were telling it, changing details and names. But without changing Hassiba's name. I dreamed that I listened to the tale, or perhaps someone in the plaza actually was telling it.

At times I was certain it was my story twisted into an unfaithful rumor, but later I thought it was the story of a romantic rival whose existence I was learning about by chance in the plaza. But Hassiba was undoubtedly Hassiba. I did not know what to think. Everything was shaping into a new garden to tell Hassiba, even though she was now the center of this one. Perhaps upon awakening, that is if I am not already awake, this may not seem to me an appropriate garden for Hassiba. And then I will dream about it again, another way. Because it was the hour in Mogador when lovers rouse, and all night and all day long, for a few glorious moments, they remain as one, entwined in an embrace.

This is the story told by the *halaiki*:

That April morning, when the ramparts of Mogador entered his eyes for the first time, Juan Isidro Labra sensed a new life was beginning for him in that coastal city, which seemed to levitate over the foam of the waves, as if at daybreak each breath of the sea had been transformed into walls. He saw an urban flower surface at the water's edge, where everyone else saw only rocks.

For more than twenty years, he had devoted himself to caring for gardens around the world. He was a nomad gardener. He had heard people speak of "The *Ryad* of Mogador" as one of the most amazing gardens that ever existed. He wrote an effusive letter to its creator, expressing his desire to pay a visit. He received an emotional and hospitable answer from his daughter, informing him that the Great Gardener of the *Ryad* had died recently, but she would welcome him with pleasure.

Only an hour after arriving at the port, and soon after settling into a room in the house of the Great Gardener, Hassiba was showing her father's *ryad* to the nomad gardener, very slowly, as if allowing him to marvel at each new area she revealed. Each terrace unveiled flowers he had never seen, virgin territory for his eyes. Every corridor seemed to lead nowhere, but would suddenly open onto the inviting seclusion of a corner bench facing a flower, or would give way to an unexpected panoramic view. He tasted dates whose flavors, unlike those he knew, had a hint of anise and guayaba. He opened figs that boiled inside and are used only to heat tea.

He enjoyed each nook, but always desired yet another surprise, which she would offer him with calculated flirtation. After a while, he realized that in a way she was showing him the most secret recesses of her body. An enormous measure of promise accompanied each sublime revelation. And he grasped intuitively the underlying meaning of his visit.

He kissed her under the shade of the orange trees. An intense sign in Hassiba's silence indicated that it was there that her mouth hoped to meet his. His hands and kisses rained softly over Hassiba's pregnant body, making her quiver, then calming her with more kisses. He undressed her

169

as slowly as they had wandered the gardens, without haste, but with ardent desire, to the pace of wonder.

When at last the nomad gardener, with his imagination tinged green, his earthy sensibility, and his hands skilled at grafting, unveiled Hassiba's sex and gazed in amazement upon her full vaginal lips, opened as if unfolding toward him, he could not help but transform them into a flower, into the most extraordinary flower he had ever seen in the world.

Hassiba's lips had always been plump, as noticeably large as the other lips that graced her face were small. But her pregnancy had made them grow, not only in size, but especially in sensitivity. A light touch moistened them and even the memory of a gentle puff transformed them into swelling waves. They had turned capricious as well, dramatically expressive, and extremely fickle. They were prone to crave something longingly, and would summon Hassiba's entire body at will, including the thin lips that suddenly acted like twins of the lower ones, lubricating more than kissing, absorbing more than biting, no longer able to pronounce anything but those nocturnal, somnambulate gestures of desire.

And as the night possessed the body and soul of those lips between her cheeks, the others, between her legs, glistened like solar beings, like a plant with pulpy leaves and petals stretching toward the light and warmth of the sun in the indisputable moment of its greatest splendor. Unique flower: zenith of the body and body of the zenith. Nothing would ever be the same for the eyes, nose, and touch of that gardener. Caressing that flower with his gaze and his fingers, he was hypnotized by it, and drawn closer and closer to it, slowly, very slowly. And even when he closed his eyes, he heard that flower growing toward him, with its music of saliva, of suspended breath.

Hassiba also sensed, but clearly in a different way, something remarkable about the mouth of her sex at that precise instant. As if her entire being, after years of searching, had finally discovered an incantation that only her vertical lips could pronounce. As if now her body had surpassed its own limits, transforming her into something more than herself. Hassiba overflowing the veins of her lips, Hassiba enlarged, Hassiba beyond known limits. Her desire was a torrent of surging blood totally submerging her in the rhythm of raucous drums beneath her skin. A tempest of beats marked the absolute possession of each of her movements and all of her thoughts.

Neither of them could know with certainty what they were to the other. Each arrived there after navigating different sensations. Though both throbbed to the same cadence, he saw that unique flower open wider and wider, as if ravenous, while Hassiba perceived her body as the increasingly rapid and thirsty solo of a drum.

She felt her slightest and most powerful transformations. Her entire body converted into the sound of a passion that flowed like a tributary, joining the sounds of her new lover, the traveling gardener. Flower and river. That is what they were without realizing it. Two different natures that meet and inadvertently unite in the blissful synchronism of a palpitation. Forces of nature transformed by each lover's gaze, transformed by the convergence of their heartbeats.

For several months, Hassiba had been undergoing a daily metamorphosis in another way. With her passion for ceramics, she imagined her pregnancy was *the invisible hand of the potter* molding her, clumsily at times and without patience, but always with an obsessive concern for the destiny of his forms. She considered herself an object of clay, sometimes pleasing, other times not at all. She had observed her body growing slowly, the way a vessel on the wheel gradually acquires a pronounced roundness. *Tide of nine moons.* The skin over her belly stretched smoothly yet demanding lotions and caresses, especially above the groin. *Like a tent inflated by the desert wind.* The skin of her buttocks became tight in some areas and loose in others. *Like rivers and lagoons converging.* Her navel asserted itself obstinately as the center and visible knot of the universe. *Where everything ties and unties.* A new stream of dark hairs traveled from the summit of her navel to the Mount of Venus. *Cascade of shadows.* The base of her spine widened, accompanied by the pain of inexperienced bones, as if she were about to sprout small intrusive wings. *Morpho butterfly discovering for the first time that it is shimmering blue.* A new substance, rougher and darker, took possession each night of her nipples, as if sensing its calling to inhabit the somnolent darkness of a mouth. *Before his work is complete, the potter inserts a handful of shadow inside the vessel.*

Now she is taut and soft at the same time, shaped by new textures. She craves and does not desire, she feels agile and clumsy, vulnerable and strong, brave and timid, alert and drowsy, hungry and nauseated, beautiful and not quite so.

Hassiba had seen how her ceramist lover had changed her into another, so much that at times only she knew that she was still herself. She was newly born to the sex and body of her lover. She was a new world, all of her, as if invisible fields sown by her transformations spread beyond her skin. She was a growing garden. And now only he could see it, feel it, enter it. Only he knew how the garden was ruled by that solar flower, the hypnotic flower of her sex, which his mouth was slowly approaching.

Let me be that nomad gardener whose hands touch you like those of that potter. Let me enter the story they tell about us and come take part in it with me. Fill yourself with me through my words, through my dreams that wish to know yours.

And the new *halaiki* of Mogador was ending his round of stories, nine times nine, narrating boldly, behind masks, his life as a gardener. Preparing himself that day to tell Hassiba a new one. Because now it was the hour in Mogador when lovers meet to tell stories.

The *halaiki*, who wishes to be called "The Gardener," always refuses to reveal if Hassiba was seduced and taken by his stories, or if only he was seduced by Hassiba's world, taken to always say yes when it is no, to desire in a labyrinthine manner, and tell stories that same way.

From this moment on, we no longer know anything: not what is real, not what is invented, not even if it is worth spinning tattered tales, even though in his audience there may be devotees who cherish them and listeners who despise them. He ravels and unravels and keeps spinning . . . He thinks of nothing but the story he will tell Hassiba that very night. It was for her that he became a voice, the earthy voice of desire. Listen as it begins anew. Because it was the hour in Mogador when lovers rouse.

Where do the stories that are told in the plaza end? Perhaps in those of us who listen to them and make them ours.

Minimal Gardener's Note and Acknowledgments

Traveling nurtures a gardener
more than any wise treatise
on gardening.
Gilles Clément

Though not exactly books of journalistic testimony, my novels include stories, passions, and pulsations that various women have told me. This one, like my other poetic explorations of desire (*The Names of the Air* and *On Lips of Water*), grew from that confidence. It was the eroticism of many pregnant women and the complexity of desire in that special moment that unleashed this particular story.

In order to write this book, it was also necessary for me to search the world for those exceptional places where nature fuses with the sensual, often extravagant imagination of certain impassioned gardeners. All the gardens in this book, either directly or indirectly, are the product of a true passion, albeit delirious. None were invented by me. I tell them, but others have put them in this world. I visited more than five hundred fascinating gardens and read about approximately one hundred more. Not all of them appear here, but all have nurtured these pages. Many people have helped and accompanied me during those years of that quest, and I thank them, although I can mention only a few.

First and foremost, Margarita de Orellana, as if there could be a garden that together we did not explore, from the Chilean Patagonia to the Kew Gardens of London, with the Sahara Desert in between. The pregnancies we shared so intensely are also in this story. My children, Andrea and Santiago, have wandered with us the most amazing tropical rainforests of Central America to the most rational gardens of France, including the forests and glaciers of Canada's Rocky Mountains. I dedicate this book to them because, in a very indirect way, aspects of all our adventures appear in its pages.

With Maricarmen Castro we visited the classic gardens of France, from Villandry to Giverny, as well as the most daring and imaginative gardens of the International Festival of Gardens in Chaumont sur Loire. *The Minimal Garden of Stones in the Wind* and *The Garden of Flowers and their Echoes* came literally from there.

For seven years, Glenn and Teri Jampol have not ceased to surprise me with the most exuberant gardens of every species of exotic flowers in Costa Rica, even those found in their own Finca Rosa Blanca. With them and their children, Olivia and Lily, we explored the amazing gardens of symbols in the Sacred Valley of Peru. Nina Subin and Eliot Weinberger, and their children Anna Della and Stephan, have undertaken intense tropical expeditions with us for more than a decade.

Oumama Aouad Lahrech invited me once again to

Mogador and opened for me the gates of her family's ancient *ryad* in Salé. To her, Tahar Lahrech, Katia and André Azoulay, Francisco Cruz, Mohamed Ennaji, and my translator to Arabic Fatiha Benlabbah, the narrator of this book owes a good many of the gardens that unlocked the heart of Hassiba. *The Garden of Traveling Cacti* is a real Mexican garden in Mogador created by the Canadian writer Scott Symons, author of *Helmet of Flesh.*

The Garden of No Return was inspired by the incredible work of fantastic architecture by León R. Zahar, and *Paradise in a Box* by his passion for the art of marquetry and its talented Mogadorian craftsmen. Both gardens, in slightly different versions, were prologues to books of his published by *Artes de México.* Inspiration for *The Garden of the Invisible* came from the pharmacies in the Moroccan markets, as well as *Flowers of the Soul,* the photographic project of Patricia Lagarde, also published by *Artes de México.*

Rhonda Buchanan showed me the equine gardens of Kentucky with their blue grass and blossoming springtime flowers during my first visit there, arranged by Manuel Medina. Danny Anderson showed me gardens in Kansas, including Calder's classic one and the garden of cricket boxes in the art museum of the city, the source for my *Garden of Voices.*

Nancy Peters, my editor at City Lights in San Francisco, took me to see the California Redwoods for the first time. Christian Duverger plunged us into the extremely wild nature of French Guayana and opened the doors to the ruins of the horrifying prison gardens on Devil's Island and the surrounding isles.

With Pilar Climent and Juan José Bremer, we visited palace gardens and ancient harems in Samarkand and Bujara, the luminous birch tree forests of Moscow, and the fanciful and delirious gardens of Peter the Great in St. Petersburg.

With Alfonso Alfaro, we explored all the gardens of Paris, and once again, with more attention, those of Mogador. Luis Ignacio Henares and Rafael López Guzmán invited us to see the gardens of Granada, from the Karmens of the Albaicín to the Alhambra, and including the exceptional garden of Manuel Rodríguez Acosta.

A Woven Ritual Garden can actually be found in the Archeological Museum of Chile, which I discovered thanks to Luz María Williamson and Roberto Edwards. John King took me to see the gardens of Lewis Carroll in Oxford. Natalia Gil showed me Newton's gravity garden and other key gardens of Cambridge, and told me about her own in India.

The Garden of Clouds and *The Cannibal Garden* are a blend of real experiences with gardens documented by Gilles Clément in his exhibition *Le Jardin Planétaire.* The gardens that I visited in books require their own acknowledgment elsewhere. The bibliography on that subject is vast and very interesting.

This book was written, rewritten, and mostly unwritten in many places and thanks to many institutions. The Banff Centre for the Arts, in Canada, where for several years I have been a conference participant, invited author, and chairman of a program for writers; Stanford University, where I have served as a Visiting Tinker Foundation Professor in the Center for Latin American Studies; and the National Foundation for Mexican Creators, of which I was a member while I wrote this book and a few others.

Like the two previous novels of this series, this one was illustrated by the master calligrapher Hassan Massoudy. His calligraphy comes mainly from his books *The Lost Garden, Calligraphy of the Earth,* and *The Journey of a Calligrapher,* and those created especially for the French edition of *On Lips of Water.* I thank him again for his warm generosity.

Alberto

THE CALLIGRAPHIC GARDEN
OF HASSAN MASSOUDY

 Hasten slowly.

It is your fear that frightens me.

"Wisdom is not in reason, but in love."
André Gide

The lost garden.

 A balance.

"The wind is lifting. Dare to live."
Paul Valéry

"If what you are about to say is not more beautiful than silence, remain quiet."
Arabic Proverb

You will give birth with pain.

 Of love and hope.

Of fear and anxieties.

 Toward our own abysses.

Journey, if you wish to grow. Remember that only by wandering the heavens the waning moon became full.

 We go.

The future.

 We are the garden.

 A shared destiny.

 They moved on.

 A sweet stillness.

Together they gave birth to this human race.

 On the way.

About the Author

Alberto Ruy-Sánchez (1951) is a fiction and non-fiction writer, poet and essayist from Mexico City. He received his doctorate in 1980 from the University Paris under the directorship of Roland Barthes. His novels offer an exploration of the many facets of desire, and nearly all his works of fiction take place in Mogador, ancient name for the Arabic city of Essaouira on the Atlantic coast of Morocco, a walled labyrinth of winding streets, marketplaces, bathhouses, and hidden gardens. His novels include: *Los nombres del aire* (1987, Premio Xavier Villaurrutia), *Los demonios de la lengua* (1987), *En los labios del agua* (1996, recipient of the Prix des Trois Continents for its French translation by Gabriel Iaculli), *Los jardines secretos de Mogador: Voces de tierra* (2001, Premio Cálamo la Otra Mirada), and *La mano del fuego* (2007). Other recent publications include: *Limulus. Visiones del fósil viviente/Visions of the Living Fossil* (2004, co-authored with the artist Brian Nissen and translated by Rhonda Dahl Buchanan) and *Nueve veces el asombro* (2005, English translation by Rhonda Dahl Buchanan, forthcoming by White Pine Press). His fiction has been translated to many languages and he spends much of his time traveling around the world as an invited lecturer and storyteller. He has published widely in scholarly journals and is the author of several books of literary criticism, including *Una introducción a Octavio Paz* (1990, recipient of the Premio José Fuentes

Mares). Since 1988, he has served as the editor-in-chief of *Artes de México*, which has won more than one hundred national and international editorial awards. In 2000 he was proclaimed *Officier de l'Ordre des Arts et des Lettres* by the French government, and in 2005 he received the honor of *Gran Orden de Honor Nacional al Mérito Autoral* in Mexico City. He is also an Honorary Citizen of Louisville, Kentucky, an Honorable Kentucky Colonel, and an Honorary Captain of the majestic steamship, the Belle of Louisville. In addition, he has served as a Visiting Tinker Scholar at Stanford University and as the Chairman of Creative Non-Fiction Program at the Banff Centre for the Arts and is a Guggenheim Fellow. Visit www.albertoruy-sanchez.com for more information about the author and his works.

About the Translator

Rhonda Dahl Buchanan is a Professor of Spanish and Director of Latin American and Latino Studies at the University of Louisville. In 2000 she received the University of Louisville Distinguished Teaching Professor Award. In 2004 she received the University of Louisville's Trustees Award and also an award to participate in a residency program at the International Banff Centre for Literary Translation in Banff, Canada, to translate Alberto Ruy-Sánchez's novel *Los jardines secretos de Mogador: Voces de la tierra.* She is the author of numerous articles on contemporary Latin American writers, and the editor of a book of critical essays, *El río de los sueños: Aproximaciones críticas a la obra de Ana María Shua* (Washington, D.C.: Interamer Collection of the Organization of American States; No. 70, 2001.) She has also translated *Limulus: Visiones del fósil viviente* (México: Artes de México, 2004), a book by Brian Nissen and Alberto Ruy-Sánchez, and is the recipient of a 2006 NEA Literature Fellowship for the translation of *Los jardines secretos de Mogador.* Her translation, *The Entre Ríos Trilogy: Three Novels* by Perla Suez was published in 2006 by The University of New Mexico Press in their Jewish Latin America Series. In 2008, her translation *Quick Fix: Sudden Fiction,* a bilingual anthology of short short stories by Ana María Shua, with illustrations by Luci Mistratov, was published by White Pine Press.

About the Calligrapher

Hassan Massoudy is an exceptional calligrapher with an international reputation. Born in 1944 in Najaf, in southern Iraq, he began his apprenticeship as a calligrapher in Baghdad. In 1969 he left Iraq to live in exile in France, where he studied at the Ecole des Beaux-Arts in Paris. In 1975, he retuned to the art of calligraphy, fusing traditional and modern elements in his work. He is an innovative artist who works as a craftsman and master teacher in his studio. He is also an avid reader and prolific writer, having published more than twenty books about the art of calligraphy. In addition, he has collaborated with musicians, singers, and dancers in performances that incorporate his calligraphies. To view examples of his calligraphies, performances, and a complete list of his books, which have been published in many languages, visit his website at www.massoudy.net. Massoudy's calligraphies form an integral part of the cycle of novels by Alberto Ruy-Sánchez that take place in Mogador. The editors of White Pine Press, Alberto Ruy-Sánchez, and Rhonda Dahl Buchanan would like to express their sincere gratitude to Hassan Massoudy for granting permission to use his calligraphies to illustrate *The Secret Gardens of Mogador: Voices of the Earth.*

COMPANIONS FOR THE JOURNEY SERIES

Inspirational work by well-known writers in a small-book format
designed to be carried along on your journey through life.

Majestic Nights

Love Poems of Bengali Women

Translated by Carolyne Wright and co-translators

VOLUME 16   978-1-893996-93-9   108 PAGES $15.00

Dropping the Bow

Poems from Ancient India

Translated by Andrew Schelling

VOLUME 15   978-1-893996-96-0   128 PAGES $15.00

White Crane

Love Songs of the Sixth Dalai Lama

Translated by Geoffrey R. Waters

VOLUME 14   1-893996-82-4   86 PAGES $14.00

Haiku Master Buson

Translated by Edith Shiffert and Yuki Sawa

VOLUME 13   1-893996-81-6   256 PAGES $16.00

The Shape of Light

Prose Pieces by James Wright

VOLUME 12   1-893996-85-9   96 PAGES $14.00

Simmering Away: Songs from the Kanginshu

Translated by Yasuhiko Moriguchi and David Jenkins

Illustrations by Michael Hofmann

VOLUME 11   1-893996-49-2   70 PAGES $14.00

10,000 Dawns: The Love Poems of Claire and Yvan Goll
Translated by Thomas Rain Crowe and Nan Watkins
VOLUME 3   1-893996-27-1   88 PAGES $13.00

There Is No Road: Proverbs by Antonio Machado
Translated by Mary G. Berg and Dennis Maloney
VOLUME 2   1-893996-66-2   118 PAGES $14.00

Wild Ways: Zen Poems of Ikkyu
Translated by John Stevens
VOLUME 1   1-893996-65-4   152 PAGES $14.00